"I am here," calle             
bedroom. You are

"Your bedroom now, my sweet. I hope I've moved all my belongings. I thought I might frighten you if I used my key, so. . . . May I come up?"

"Are you alone?"

"Yes, I am alone."

"I'll come down. Will you have a drink? Or if you'd like coffee, please tell Meggie."

"Coffee, Meggie!" Patrick shouted. "I say, Emily, how you've grown."

She had brushed her hair before going to bed, and now she wasn't tired at all. It must be something to do with the atmosphere of vitality that Patrick had brought into the house. He stood looking up at her, his thin face tilted at an appraising angle, his blue eyes keen with interest, his reddish hair slightly long, very thick and curly, very decorative. His clothes were casual and obviously expensive. He looked expensive altogether. Patrick Lloyd, baronet, exceedingly attractive, and fully aware of it.

But there was something about him that disturbed her. . . .

Dorothy Eden

# THE HOUSE
## on
# HAY HILL

A FAWCETT CREST BOOK

Fawcett Publications, Inc., Greenwich, Connecticut

Acknowledgment is made to *Good Housekeeping* and *Woman's Journal*, where these stories first appeared.

# *Contents*

# THE HOUSE
### *on*
# HAY HILL

# The House on Hay Hill

They remembered Emily when she checked into the Connaught, that small and highly individual hotel in London's fashionable Mayfair district. Or at least they gave the good-mannered impression that they did, for she had been only 12 years old the time she stayed there with her mother, nearly ten years ago. But then, of course, they had known her great-aunt, everyone in London did . . . and quite a few on the Continent as well.

"Good afternoon, Miss Armitage. How nice to see you again. Will you be staying with us long?"

"No, only one or two nights, I expect." She couldn't resist communicating her excitement. "I've inherited a house. I have to see how soon I can live in it. I'm going there now to have a look at it." Her joy lit up her face and warmed her cheeks. "It was Lady Lloyd's, my great-aunt's," she added.

"Ah, Lady Lloyd. Indeed, indeed. She always came here to Sunday luncheon. She was a great lady."

A great lady. Yes, and a real character, Emily thought. Generous, wayward, impulsive, headstrong, acquisitive, arrogant, *spectacular*. The kind of *grande dame* that only the English really produced well. Someone who might have thought her great-niece, Emily Armitage, aged 12, blonde, serious and fearfully shy, scarcely worth noticing or remembering. But she had noticed. And remembered.

For the house on Hay Hill, with all of its magpie contents, had been left to Emily. Its value, Mr. Brinsley, the attorney, wrote—solicitor, he had called himself—was some 200,000 pounds, somewhere in the neighborhood of 500,000 American dollars. The contents had not yet been appraised. Perhaps Emily would let him have her instructions about selling. He had no doubt she would want everything put on the market.

"Nothing to be sold," Emily firmly cabled from Boston. "Arriving London end of month."

She couldn't come sooner because she had to give two weeks' notice to the accounting firm for which she worked. Nothing could please her more than giving up her boring job!

Now she would never have to work again, her mother had said. She could sell the house, invest the capital and live comfortably for the rest of her life.

But that was not what Emily wanted.

What her great-aunt had in mind might have been

something entirely different. No one really knew Aunt Emilia, that chameleon whose matrimonial life had been, to say the least, varied. Had she thought Emily, that tongue-tied and blundering child she'd met only once would have difficulty finding herself a husband?

Emily wished her aunt could have known otherwise. She had her share of beaux—Aunt Emilia would have liked that choice of words—plenty of them: Jim Robertson, a professor of history at Boston U., for example; and Harvey Lester, blond as the sun and a crack tennis player; and Jud Henderman and Peter Tate and . . . .

Obviously, she had genuinely liked her great-niece and namesake. Hadn't she sent her gifts from everywhere?— a green and gold mandarin robe from Hong Kong; a string of sky-blue worry beads from Greece; a Dutch-made tape recorder so that neither of them would have to write, simply send nice chatty tapes back and forth across the Atlantic; and a beautiful leather pocketbook from Florence.

What fun it had been to get a tape of Emilia's voice recounting in its own cadence and enthusiasm this or that marvelous event—"Last evening, dear girl, we attended the Royal Ballet at Covent Garden, a benefit for the Children's Hospital, and that exquisite young Russian leaped across the stage like a stag in flight. . . ."

Aunt Emilia, her mother had told her, had always wanted a daughter but had only boys, one by her second marriage and one by her third. She had been in her forties when her last son, Patrick, was born, and shortly afterwards, her last marriage, the one that had given her the title, had ended in divorce.

She had been a lonely woman, her mother said, when

she and Emily had visited Aunt Emilia in London. But Emily had been unable to imagine that flamboyant, imperious old lady ever being lonely. Emily had thought her fascinating and wholly admirable, and her narrow house wedged between two larger ones on Hay Hill had been a treasure chest. Inheriting the house had been the most unexpected and fantastic thing that had ever happened to Emily. Of course she had no intention of selling it. She intended to live in it.

She wouldn't stop now to unpack. It was already late and she must go and see the house—her house—before dark. If there were no one there she would have to be content to stand outside. It was Saturday, and Mr. Brinsley would not be in his office. She would have to wait until Monday to get the keys. But she could look.

Her handbag slung over her shoulder, she stepped outside into the dusk.

The doorman saluted her. "Taxi, miss?"

"No, thank you. I think I'll walk."

"Mind how you go now. Mayfair isn't what it used to be. We've our share of muggers about these days, too."

She nodded and went on her way down the narrow, quiet streets, past the small luxury shops—antiques, china, lingerie, picture galleries—past the glossy doorways of expensive houses with polished door knockers and bay trees in tubs; past the red telephone booths, the small church with its austere spire; and past red stucco and old mellowed soot-stained brick to the row of houses on the gentle incline called Hay Hill.

Berkeley Square lay on one side, Park Lane on the other. That quaint, ancient labyrinth of streets called Shepherd Market was just beyond.

Rich houses and poor houses. Emily breathed deeply. This square mile of old London was soaked in history. Hadn't Becky Sharp, the heroine of *Vanity Fair*—one of her favorite characters in English literature—lived near here? Well, as much as Sherlock Holmes had lived in Baker Street.

Aunt Emilia's house, narrow as a gray spinster between two rather plump brick-faced dowagers, was exactly as Emily remembered it, even to the faded red paint of the door.

And what good luck. There was a dim glow of light coming from behind drawn curtains on the second floor. That surely was the room that had been Aunt Emilia's. Emily remembered vividly its smell of attar of roses, its mirrors, its bed with sheets and pillows embroidered with handmade lace. She felt tears of emotion spring to her eyes. Her hand trembled slightly as she pressed the doorbell. She heard it ringing faintly a long way off. She waited and listened. No one came. She rang again, then rapped the heavy brass door knocker.

Why didn't somebody come?

Why didn't the person upstairs answer the door?

She stepped back to look up at the lighted window, and saw that it had gone dark. Was someone coming downstairs? No light appeared in the window over the front door. There was no sound from within. Emily put her ear against the door and listened. Silence. Or could she hear a cat mewing? She peered through the flap of the letter box and saw only darkness.

Had she imagined the light upstairs? Had it been only a reflection of a passing car's lights? Had it shone through from a house at the back?

She lingered, desperately disappointed and frustrated. This was her house and she couldn't get inside. She walked slowly down the stairs, thinking.

It was very strange, but she was sure there *was* someone inside. An intruder? Someone who had no right to be there and had no intention of making his or her presence known?

Measured footsteps sounded behind her.

"You looking for something, miss?" It was a policeman, a tall English bobby.

"No, there doesn't seem to be anyone at home."

"Weren't they expecting you?"

Emily shook her head.

"Well, don't loiter, miss. Odd types about nowadays."

"Thank you," she said. She supposed she looked young and naïve; and men, even policemen, liked to think she needed protection. She supposed that was nice, too.

Back at the hotel she unpacked, took a shower, dressed for dinner. The waiters in the dining room were charming to her. They gave her a pleasant table, and hovered with discreet suggestions about food and wine. The roast beef or the lamb chop, they murmured. Perhaps a half bottle of Burgundy? Their paternal gaze told her that she was pretty, that she wouldn't often be dining alone.

After dinner she would be extravagant and call Mother in Boston. But first she had a hunch to do something else, less conventional and probably quite unfruitful.

In her bedroom she looked in the telephone directory and found the listing for her aunt's house.

She thought the telephone might still be connected and asked the operator to try the number. Emily waited while the gentle birring began. The call wouldn't be answered, of course. She was only acting on a hunch that there really had been someone in Aunt Emilia's bedroom, who didn't want to answer the doorbell and be seen. But a telephone ringing usually aroused a powerful curiosity.

Even an intruder might be lured into the trap of answering it.

All the same, Emily started nervously when the telephone came alive in her hand.

"Emily Armitage speaking," said a voice that was a distinct imitation of her own. Her name, and her voice! It just couldn't be.

"*Who?*"

The astonishment with which she spoke must have warned the person at the other end of the line, for abruptly the telephone clicked and went dead.

Emily sat back, looking at the instrument in wonder and disbelief.

Had she heard correctly? That half bottle of Burgundy —she wasn't used to wine, but that mild French wine couldn't be responsible. Someone using her name, speaking in her voice.

It was impossible. She'd try the number again.

"We were cut off," she said to the operator.

But this time the birring went on and on. No one answered. Just like the light going out when she had rung the doorbell.

She was either mentally confused by the time change after the long Atlantic flight, or something very odd was going on.

And that she could not sort out at ten o'clock at night. She couldn't even call Mother now, for what was she to say? Mother recognized, and worried about, the slightest hint of alarm in her voice.

Best go to bed and sleep.

On a Sunday morning Mayfair would have lost its dangers and its mysteries. She was simply exhausted.

She was awakened by the telephone. Sleepily remembering her alarm of the previous night she snatched at the receiver.

"Emily!" A man's voice. Pleasant. Very, very English.

"Yes," she said cautiously. "Who is this?"

"I'd hardly expect you to remember me, but I'm your cousin. Barnaby Chisholm."

"Barnaby!" Of course she remembered. Every detail of that earlier visit to London was vivid. Barnaby had been a dark-haired, dark-eyed, very correct young man in his twenties. She had admired his bowler hat, his striped trousers, his neatly furled umbrella. He had been something terribly conventional in the city, a stockbroker, a banker, something like that.

Of course she remembered, and was overjoyed to hear his friendly voice.

"Barnaby, how did you know I was here?"

"Because I've been ringing the Connaught so often that finally I wore the management down. They divulged information and said you were arriving last night. Are you up?"

"No. Should I be? What's the time?"

"It's ten o'clock on the Sabbath and I'm coming round to have breakfast with you. In half an hour."

"Really! How nice!" Belatedly she added, "What about your wife? Or am I—I mean, I expect—"

"You mean have I got one, and the answer is no. I'm

38 and a confirmed bachelor secretly wanting to be unconfirmed."

"I'll be downstairs in 30 minutes flat."

"What a loss," said Barnaby, 35 minutes later, holding both of Emily's hands and looking at her with his probing, rather somber eyes, which she found she remembered quite accurately. His middle had thickened a little, which suited him. Not good-looking, but attractive in a dogged sort of way. The same serious Barnaby.

"What do you mean?"

"If Mother's eldest sister—your grandmother—had married an Englishman instead of an American you would be English. And wouldn't that be nice for all of us?"

Dear, staid old Barnaby; his gaze was blatantly admiring. "You have grown up nicely, Emily. It's wonderful to see you."

"I thought . . . I worried that perhaps . . . I mean, you and Patrick might resent that your mother left her house to me. . . ."

"Nonsense! She hoped you'd live here. She knew you'd adore it. And let's be fair—Mother has treated both of us pretty well. She started me in a business which I can modestly say has flourished."

"And Patrick?"

"Oh, he gets along, though don't ask me how. He's rather the playboy. You know, sports cars and that sort of thing."

Emily laughed, trying to remember Patrick. Someone pink-cheeked, blue-eyed, terribly restless. He hadn't been patient with a schoolgirl, as Barnaby had.

"You say that as if it were a deadly sin," she said.

Barnaby shrugged.

"You've grown up nicely, too," she said a little later.

"You mean aged?"

"Don't be silly. I can't think why you haven't married, though. You look awfully eligible. What about Patrick?"

"I think Mother's variegated career has slightly put both of us off marriage. Patrick has a slim elegant creation called a Jaguar as a wife. At least, that was his state at the time of Mother's funeral."

"Only six weeks ago. Is he likely to have changed that status since?"

"Who knows? The lady may be a new bright-red Aston Martin now. Or whatever. I know little about cars. We're only half brothers, you know. Even as full brothers I doubt if we'd have been close. I'm frankly nervous of fast cars, and Patrick thinks bills and debentures and all that boring, to say the least. Do I look like an investment banker?"

"I don't know, I've never met one. But, yes." Emily noticed again the serious face, the glossy hair, the well-cut gray-flannel suit, the unobtrusive tie. "I should think you do. I like it," she added sincerely. "You look just the way I expect an Englishman to look. Distinguished and clever and responsible."

"Really?" His smile was faintly lugubrious. "Well, I am approaching 40. A successful man should be all those things by then."

"And Patrick?"

"Patrick doesn't confide in me. Let's say his *exterior* is very stylish."

"But one doesn't know what's behind it?"

"No."

"Interesting," Emily murmured.

"And he has inherited the title, of course."

"Sir Patrick. Well." Emily caught a look on Barnaby's face. Envy that he hadn't been the eldest son of Sir Francis Lloyd—Aunt Emilia's last husband—and not that of Mr. Justice Chisholm who had only been eminent, learned and rich? She tactfully changed the subject. "Ah, here's the coffee!"

The company of Barnaby had the welcome effect of reducing the disturbing mystery of last night to something that could now be spoken of lightly.

"By the way, is anyone living in Aunt Emilia's house? I walked to Hay Hill last night to gloat over my property, and I thought I saw a light upstairs, although no one answered the door."

"Probably did see a light."

"I did?"

"Meggie's there. You remember Meggie? No, I don't believe you ever met her. She came to Mother after Kate left about eight years ago."

"Well, if Meggie, whoever she is, was there, why didn't she answer?"

"Because she's deaf. She spends most of the day in the basement beside the kitchen fire, with her cat, an ugly monster called Patch."

"Goodness, she sounds like a witch."

"A Welsh witch, no less. Megan Owen. I'm afraid you've inherited her. House and contents, wasn't it? Meggie is very much contents. Immovable." He patted her hand. "But don't look so worried. If she likes you, she'll be a perfect servant."

Emily said sadly, "I had thought of getting one of those

big woolly sheepdogs. You know, with Shepherd Market so close, it seemed appropriate. But if there's a cat. . . ."

"He'll fill the place of a watchdog admirably, I would say."

Emily laughed.

"A deaf old woman and a cat and I was scared. Would you believe it? But that cop. . . ."

"Policeman."

"Okay, policeman. He warned me not to 'linger in the streets after dark.' "

"Quite right, too."

"But, Barnaby, there was something else. When I called the house later, just to see if there had been a light in that upstairs window, someone did answer the telephone but it couldn't have been old Meggie. For one thing, if she's stone deaf she wouldn't have heard it, and for another the voice was young. In fact," she crumbled her toast nervously, "it was an American voice, like mine. Whoever it was said she *was* me."

Barnaby's eyes were quizzical.

"Really, I know it sounds strange, but. . . ."

"Surely you must have misunderstood."

"No. Even before I spoke, whoever it was said, 'Emily Armitage speaking' as though she were expecting someone to call, someone for whom she was waiting."

"You must have gotten a wrong number. There's an awful lot of that lately and perhaps you were overly tired from your flight. It couldn't be, Emily. You just thought you heard. . . ."

"Perhaps," she said. "Maybe after my seeing the light and all. . . . But still. . . ."

"We English have our ghosts, as you know. . . ."

She smiled. "But they don't appear over the telephone."

"I suspect the hotel operator said that Miss Emily Armitage was calling and whoever answered repeated it. That's reasonable, isn't it? In the form of a query? Emily Armitage? I'm sure that's what happened."

"Barnaby, what a logical mind you have!"

"Let's get it straightened out thoroughly," Barnaby said. "We'll go round to the house this morning."

"But I haven't a key. I'm to see Mr. Brinsley tomorrow to get one."

"I have one. So has Patrick, for that matter, and he had some personal stuff he was moving. I say . . . I wonder if. . . ."

"What?"

"Just a thought. Never mind."

Emily leaned forward. "I know exactly what you're thinking. That Patrick might have a girl friend. She might even be American, mightn't she? And if Meggie's that deaf. . . ."

Barnaby's brows drew together in a deep frown.

"Not in my mother's house, I hope," he said, then smiled reluctantly. "Heaven knows, Mother wasn't that strong on morals. I was only a schoolboy at the time she divorced father, but I remember being outraged and horribly shocked. Still, she was my mother, and I was fond of her, and that *was* her house. It speaks of her. You know the clutter of things she surrounded herself with, valuable and worthless, but uniquely Mother's taste. I wouldn't have thought Patrick would have the bad taste to take a girl there. If he did."

"You don't approve of Patrick either, do you Barnaby?" Emily asked lightly.

"No. But I expect you will. All girls do."

"If he's the playboy you say he is, I won't. I'm a serious person. I don't just plan to live in London for fun. I'm going to take archaeology classes. I've always wanted to be an archaeologist. I'm crazy about old things."

Now Barnaby was smiling benevolently. "And you look as fresh as a newly minted coin yourself. Well, then, the time has come to begin a dig through your inheritance."

The cat, an enormous black and white creature with a tail like a feather duster, rubbed against Emily's legs as she went down the steep narrow stairs to the basement.

She could hear Barnaby shouting, "I've brought Miss Armitage to see you, Meggie. Emily Armitage. Mother's great-niece."

"American?" said a surly disapproving voice. "How did Madam think I could live with an American?"

"More to the point, Meggie, how is Emily going to live with you?" Barnaby's voice was meant to be chaffing, but he shouted as if he were cheering at a baseball game.

Emily wasn't surprised by the dark look she got from the tiny old lady seated by a glowing fire. The mantelpiece was cluttered with chipped and cracked china figures, but the low-ceilinged room was spotlessly clean as was the colored rag mat in front of the fire. The little rocking chair and the cat's basket gave an air of coziness and welcome that almost overcame Meggie's hostility.

Emily held out her hand. "I'm so glad to meet you, Meggie."

The cat, which had followed her down the stairs, rubbed vigorously around her ankles.

Meggie looked Emily up and down with a pair of small eyes as black and shiny as the well-polished grate.

"How do you do, miss. I suppose you're wondering how to get rid of me."

"Nothing of the sort," said Emily.

"Now, Meggie, you're being wicked," Barnaby shouted. "Miss Emily has no intention of getting rid of you."

"Well, tell her I don't know how to cook hamburgers, and I'm too old to learn."

Poor thing, she's probably worried sick, Emily thought, as she tried to assure Meggie she would always have a home.

"Don't let Meggie upset you," Barnaby said, following Emily upstairs. "She makes a practice of being deliberately rude. It's her hobby. She enjoys people's reactions. Actually, she liked you."

"How could you possibly tell?"

"The hamburger bit was meant to be a joke. She only jokes with people she likes."

"Heaven help me!" Emily sighed, then giggled. "Don't worry, we'll get on all right."

The entered the drawing room, a long, narrow room that ran the width of the house, its window looking onto the street and over the courtyard at the back. It was a small Aladdin's cave, full of pictures, porcelain, gilt and enamel ornaments, silver candlesticks, gleaming satinwood and mahogany furniture that was surely Chippendale, and faded old rose and blue rugs.

"I remember it," Emily said in a hushed voice. "But not so many things. Surely not so many."

"I agree. In the last few years collecting went to Mother's head. A few of her acquisitions were genuine treasures, but mostly they were just Victorian bric-a-brac."

"There used to be a little gilt clock with cherubs on the mantelpiece. It was decorated with garlands of roses on sky-blue enamel."

"It was French," said Barnaby. "Rather nice. I don't remember seeing it around lately. But Mother moved things, or sold them. Dealers used to come pestering her. She was well known in auction rooms."

"Mr. Brinsley will have a list of everything?"

"Yes, indeed. It all had to be valued for estate taxes."

"I hope the clock is tucked away someplace. My mother admired it when we were here and I thought I'd make her a birthday present of it."

"Let's look in the other rooms. There's so much." Barnaby picked up a porcelain shepherdess and put it down. "I'm surprised you even remember the clock."

"I was only 12, and I certainly wasn't interested in dark, old pictures. I remember the clock chiming and thinking it charming, and I guess Mother's liking it so much. . . ."

In the bedroom, the four-poster bed, with its brocade spread, looked sadly unoccupied. On the ornate dressing table were silver-backed brushes and mirrors, crystal perfume bottles, and several photographs of Emily during various stages of her growth—all in little silver frames. She hadn't known Aunt Emilia had cared so much. Besides that array was a jewel box filled with fake and semiprecious jewelry—crystal beads, some amethysts and carnelians, a bracelet set with agates, pearls that were obviously imitation.

"The real stuff is in the bank," Barnaby said. "Mother had some rather nice pieces. You'll be able to get them out."

Emily was opening the wardrobe. She had a curious sense of restlessness and uneasiness.

The smell of attar of roses was very strong as she swished through the clothes—brocade and velvet evening gowns, day dresses, coats.

"Do I have to get rid of all this?"

"Give it to some worthy charity. Or, I daresay, some repertory theater could use it."

"Isn't there a bedroom here that isn't full of Aunt Emilia?"

"The one at the back that Patrick sometimes uses. I live in my own flat in London—in Victoria—but his house is down in Surrey. He used to spend the night when he came to see Mother. I dined with her once a week."

Barnaby, the good but rather dull son; Patrick, the selfish but undoubtedly more amusing one. At least that was what a woman like Aunt Emilia would think.

Emily took Barnaby's arm.

"May I see the room, please? I don't actually want to sleep in Aunt Emilia's until I redo it."

He led her to a small room with a narrow bed, white coverlet, small military chest, leather chair, some old prints of birds on the wall.

She was thinking of Patrick in this room, a vague boyish ghost with that reddish hair she remembered. Hopefully, he wouldn't resent her moving in. He'd understand that she couldn't move into his mother's room just yet, not until some memories were banished.

"Barnaby, this will do beautifully. I'll move in today."

"Really! Don't be too impulsive. Shouldn't you wait to see Brinsley first? And have this room done up a bit? It's not very feminine."

"No, I won't change a thing. And I intend to move today. I can't wait. I love it all too much."

"Well, I don't know. Rather you than me. The whole place needs airing."

"Then let's open some windows."

"Good idea. Then it's time for lunch. We'll go to the Ritz."

"The Ritz. Barnaby, are you a millionaire?"

"For you, and your first visit in a decade, yes."

"How sweet! I'm so glad you're here."

They went outside and Emily looked up at her house with a new pride of ownership. That it should happen to her. It was like a fairy tale.

Later that afternoon, in spite of his amiability and his obvious determination not to interfere, Barnaby did think her move rather hasty. But if she'd made her mind up. . . .

"While I think of it," Barnaby said, "let me give you my address and telephone number. You can get me any time of the day or night. If I'm not there, my secretary, Miss Hopwood, will be."

"In your apartment?" Emily asked. She remembered Miss Hopwood's name from her previous visit.

"In my flat." Barnaby grinned. "Nothing immoral—I have my office there."

"Nevertheless I expect she's madly in love with you," Emily teased.

Barnaby blushed. "Not likely."

Not unlikely at all. Barnaby, in his quiet serious way,

was an attractive man. Poor Miss Hopwood would probably like to scratch out the eyes of his women friends.
He must have women friends. He had been a perfect
host at lunch today. She had been a little bedazzled, in
that lovely restaurant at the Ritz, with its view over one
of the most beautiful parks in London. If she were not
careful, she would become addicted to luxury.

Now she must settle down in Aunt Emilia's house and
get over this walking-on-air feeling.

When she had unpacked her bags, she would pay
another visit to Meggie in the kitchen to establish a better
relationship, call Mother in Boston, then have an early
night. She would sleep well in that plain room of Patrick's.
What a strange paradox he must be, with his flashy way
of life, and this austere room.

But why had Barnaby emphasized that she could call
him at any time of the day or night? As if he expected
she might need to? Had he thought Patrick might impose
himself?

Mother's voice was as clear as if it came from the next
room.

"Baby, I've been sitting by the telephone for hours.
How are you? Did you have a good flight? Why didn't you
call me sooner?"

"Because it would have been four o'clock in the morning in Boston. And everything's fine. Wonderful. I'm in
my own house."

"Already?"

"Yes. Barnaby helped me move in. He's been marvelous."

"I'm glad it was Barnaby. He took after his father, as

I remember. Trustworthy. A bit cautious, perhaps."

"He's still cautious."

"Well, isn't that cute. I'd certainly trust him rather than the other one . . . Patrick. He was wild."

"Sir Patrick now, Mother."

"Really?" Emily heard the subtle change in her mother's voice. "Well, perhaps he's settled down."

"Not from what Barnaby says."

"That's a pity. Is either of them married?"

"Not yet. It seems as if Barnaby's too cautious, and Patrick's too wild. And don't get any ideas, Mother, because I'm going to be studying hard. And I still adore London."

"Well, my darling, take care."

"I will. I have a Welsh witch and a cat the size of a sheepdog to guard me."

"Honey, you're beginning to sound like Aunt Emilia already. Is it the house?"

"Yes," Emily said thoughtfully, "I think it is. I like it."

She was too tired after all to attempt to converse with Meggie that night. She wrote a message. *May I please have a glass of cold milk and an apple, if you have one. I'm going to bed early.* She added, *Thank you very much.* The Welsh witch must be placated.

The milk and the apple arrived on a tray, accompanied by Patch at Meggie's heels. Meggie left, her wrinkled-nut face expressionless. Patch stayed. Presently he landed on Emily's bed with a thud, and proceeded to take up three quarters of the space. Emily, though uncomfortably cramped, was glad of his company. She had been thinking the house a little too quiet, almost eerily so.

Yet what did she want, creaking stairs, ghostly whispers? A voice saying, "Emily Armitage speaking"?

The voice, as she was falling asleep, didn't say Emily Armitage, it shouted, "Meggie! Meggie!" and there was a thunderous knocking at the door.

Emily shot up in acute alarm, and Patch was gone like a flying bale of hay from her bed.

She was in her dressing gown at the top of the stairs when the front door clicked open and the deep voice called, "Meggie, your hearing's improving. I didn't have to wake the street tonight."

Meggie said something inaudible, bringing an exclamation.

"Is she now?"

"Yes, I am here," called Emily. "And occupying your bedroom. I hope you don't mind. You are Patrick, aren't you?"

"*Your* bedroom now, my sweet. I hope I've moved all my belongings. I thought I might frighten you if I used my key, so. . . . May I come up?"

"Are you alone?"

The tall figure looked around. "Do you see anyone with me?"

"No one waiting in your car?"

"Ah, ha! Old Barnaby's been talking. No, I am alone."

"I'll come down. Will you have a drink? Or if you'd like coffee, please tell Meggie."

"Coffee, Meggie!" Patrick shouted. "I say, Emily, how you've grown."

She had brushed her hair before going to bed, but luckily hadn't put it up in curlers or smothered her face with night cream. She had been too tired to do any beauty routines. Now she wasn't tired at all. It must be something to do with the atmosphere of vitality that Patrick had brought into the house. He stood looking up at her, his thin face tilted at an appraising angle, his blue eyes keen with interest, his reddish hair slightly long, very thick and curly, very decorative. His clothes were casual and obviously expensive. He looked expensive altogether. Patrick Lloyd, baronet, exceedingly attractive, and fully aware of it.

"You don't mind my being here?" she asked.

His eyebrows went up. "Do I look the sort of chap who would mind the company of a pretty girl?"

"You know what I mean." Barnaby had known at once, and been infinitely tactful. "I've inherited a rather valuable property that you might rightly think should have been yours."

"And that makes you an intruder? Albeit a delicious one? I suppose you are, in a way. Actually it had entered my head that it's going to be rather more expensive spending a night or two in town now. But I'm a great defender of personal rights. If Mother wanted you to have her house, then it's absolutely her privilege to give it to you."

"You're still welcome to stay here. I really mean that."

"I can see you do. Those innocent blue eyes. How old are you, Emily? Sixteen?"

"Do I look like a schoolgirl?" Emily asked tartly. "You know very well I'm 22."

"Oh dear! Then Meggie will have to chaperone. Never mind, she's conveniently deaf."

Conveniently? So that, tucked away in her basement, she never heard Patrick arrive with his girl friends? He surely didn't thunder at the door unless he was alone.

Now he was sauntering about the drawing room touching things.

"Extraordinary lot of junk Mother surrounded herself with. Are you going to clear it away or treasure it? No, you're much too young to need props like this." He picked up a silver candlestick and put it down. "Well, what are you going to do, Emily?"

"Live in the house. Study. I'm going to enroll in classes at London University, if they'll have me."

His blue eyes looked surprised. "You've just been assuring me you aren't a schoolgirl."

"I should think I'm a great deal more grown up than you, and you're at least eight years older. And I'm not in the first grade, Sir Patrick, I'm studying archaeology."

"Well, well! All that in that fetching little blonde head. And spunky to boot."

"Barnaby understood," Emily said stiffly.

"Oh, old Barnaby. If you're what you say, you two will get along like a house on fire. He with his stock-market reports, you with your Roman cooking pots. Get dressed and come out and have dinner with me at the Ritz."

"Barnaby took me there for lunch."

"Did he, now? Then tomorrow we'll lunch at the Mirabelle. Let him try to outdo that."

"I'm seeing Mr. Brinsley tomorrow."

"For heaven's sake, don't lunch with him. He'll give you a glass of beer and a cheese sandwich."

"That sounds fine to me, since I thought I'd take a look at the British Museum afterwards."

"Now that," said Patrick, "is my idea of a really festive day. Let's finish it by having dinner. The Mirabelle, and then a nightclub. Or do you prefer gambling?"

"Gambling!"

"There's the Curzon House Club 100 yards from here.
Mother used to love it."

Emily sighed helplessly. "I can't keep up. Aunt Emilia
gambling?"

"It was hardly like going to some den of iniquity. It's
all rather elegant, like Monte Carlo. The best of people,
the *crème de la crème*. Whatever else Mother was, she
was always first class. Except," he said, "for that ghastly
scent she used. Hopefully when you've established your
own personality here everything will be quite different."
He came closer. "You are rather ravishing. That little
head crammed with serious thoughts, and a neck like
Nefertiti's. I find it an almost irresistible combination."

"Almost?"

"I'm reserving final judgment. You might truly prefer
Roman cooking pots, and old ruins."

There was a tap on the door. Now that was significant.
Dour old Meggie, not noted for her manners, didn't enter
unannounced when handsome Sir Patrick was here. Was
she afraid of interrupting something?

"Ah, here's the coffee. Just what I need before a long
drive home."

Meggie set the tray on the table and left.

"Patrick, had you come to stay?"

"No, I was only checking on Meggie. In a curious way
I'm rather fond of the old grump. She really shouldn't be
here alone. Thugs get to know when there's an old woman
in a house full of valuables."

"Did you check last night, too?"

"No, I didn't. Why do you ask?"

"I walked over from the Connaught, and I thought I saw a light in your mother's room."

"Oh?" Those clear sharp blue eyes were looking at her.

"I must have imagined it. It was dusk. It must have been a reflection of car headlights, or something. By the way, do you remember a little gilt clock with cherubs? I've missed it. I liked its chimes."

"On the mantelpiece, wasn't it?" said Patrick. His eyes had narrowed. "Ask Mr. Brinsley. He'll know."

After that he drank his coffee rather quickly, and said that he would have to go.

"Tomorrow night, eight sharp," he said. "If the telephone rings, don't answer it."

"What do you mean?"

"What's the matter? I wasn't trying to scare you. I only know old Barnaby's quiet, deadly persuasiveness with serious-minded girls. You're not to stand me up."

"Of course, I wouldn't do that."

"But you suddenly look scared."

"What of?"

"You tell me. Being here alone?"

She found, however, that she didn't want to discuss that odd telephone call. He would only laugh. Even Barnaby had laughed—more or less.

Besides, she wasn't in the least scared now. She was rather excited, in fact. She would wear that new dress she had lost her head over, and she'd show him. Schoolgirl, indeed!

Mr. Brinsley's office belonged strictly to the Charles

Dickens era. Mr. Brinsley himself was remarkably like a Dickens character. His flushed face was plump and jolly, his eyes watery blue, spherical and twinkly. He welcomed Emily with an outstretched hand as soft as a down cushion.

"Miss Armitage! And how do you find London? Damp, foggy, dark? But wait until spring." He pinged a silver bell on his desk, making Emily jump. A middle-aged secretary—dowdy and expressionless—appeared.

"Miss Tucker, would you be good enough to bring us some tea."

"Yes, sir."

"Splendid. Miss Armitage, you wrote telling me you intended to live in your great-aunt's house. Now that you have arrived, do you still wish to do so?"

Did he mean that some happening might have made her change her mind? No, of course not. Those round eyes were blandly innocent.

"Oh, yes. More than ever!"

"Splendid. But you *do* understand that it will cost money to live in Mayfair. Rates and other charges are quite prohibitive. And an old house like that needs constant repair. I don't wish to pry, Miss Armitage, but have you an income of your own?"

"Not a penny," said Emily cheerfully. "But I plan to sell off some of the contents of the house. There's so much and it isn't all exactly my taste. Aunt Emilia did have some valuable things, didn't she?"

"Quite so."

"Barnaby said something about jewelry in the bank."

"Yes, she always kept it there. She had one or two good pieces that she used to take out when she wanted to wear them. They were always returned the next day. Her jewelry was the only thing she worried about as far as burglars were concerned. I have it all listed in the valuation made for probate purposes. Ah, here is our tea. Miss Tucker, get me the Lady Lloyd estate file."

"I only want to sell enough to support myself while I take a university course. After that, I'll think again."

"Very wise. And I agree with you that a certain number of Lady Lloyd's possessions are plain junk, even though they'll still fetch a price. She was a regular magpie, you know. Every bit of glitter attracted her. And the jewelry is very old-fashioned for a modern young lady like yourself. So let us be practical."

Mr. Brinsley put on spectacles and peered at the papers.

"Schedule B—contents of house—valuation 20,000 pounds. A conservative value. I may say. We don't give the Chancellor of the Exchequer any more than we can help in death taxes."

"Twenty thousand pounds. Why, that sounds like a fortune."

"Not so much nowadays. And you won't be disposing of the whole lot of the contents of the house, will you? Just do it gradually. They tell me prices in the auction rooms are increasing year by year. Now let me see. Jewelry, wearing apparel, etc. That includes one fine diamond and emerald ring which you may well want to keep. Your aunt took that sort of thing to Cartier's in Bond Street for cleaning and such. I'd have the setting checked, if I were you. And perhaps the ring needs to be adjusted to fit you. Your aunt was somewhat larger, you know."

"I'll do that today, first thing," Emily said, elated. "Tell me, Mr. Brinsley, did Barnaby and Patrick mind my getting all this? They said they didn't. They're terribly nice about it, but—"

"On my advice, Miss Armitage, Lady Lloyd provided for her sons some years before her death. This had the double purpose of starting them in life and avoiding death duties. They've been handsomely treated, so you don't need to worry."

"I'm so glad," Emily said.

"It was always your great-aunt's intention to remember you in her will. She took a fancy to you as a child. Reminded her of herself, she said. She liked that."

Mr. Brinsley beamed happily, and Emily felt the excitement and elation surging through her again. Now she needed to have no doubts.

Except. . . . "Can I see the list of the contents of the house, Mr. Brinsley?"

"By all means. It's rather long. I'll give you a copy to take home as you'll want time to study it. For the sale of any of the better articles I suggest Sotheby's or Christie's auction rooms. But I'd consult with your cousin Barnaby on that. He's the businessman. He has a good head on steady shoulders."

"Not Patrick?"

"That young man is something of a mystery. I know nothing of his means of support. But he always seems prosperous. However, I'm sure you have your head firmly on your shoulders, Miss Armitage."

And won't be taken in by Patrick's charm? Emily thought.

Emily smiled, but said nothing. She thought of mentioning the missing clock, then decided against doing so. It would be on the list. If it were not, then probably Aunt

Emilia had sold it or given it away.

She felt that the interview with Mr. Brinsley could not have been more satisfactory. She had the list of the contents of the house, and the authority to pick up the jewelry from the bank. As she left his office, Mr. Brinsley said, "I've spoken to the manager. And remember that I am at your service at any time. Don't hesitate to ask for advice."

The jewelry, as she had expected, was variegated. Emily knew at once that she would be selling the Victorian mourning brooches and jet beads, the garnets and amethysts in their heavy old-fashioned settings. She would keep the rope of pearls. She remembered Aunt Emilia wearing them, twisted around her slender throat, her handsome head held high. There were a dozen or so rings, but the only one of real value was the diamond and emerald one. It was rather magnificent, said the bank manager, and must be adequately insured. He, too, suggested Emily take it to Cartier's for cleaning and appraisal.

"And when you're not wearing it, Miss Armitage, do be careful where you put it. Burglaries are everyday happenings now."

"Everyone is warning me about crime," Emily complained.

"And with good reason, I'm sorry to say. The insurance company will probably want to look at the locks on your house. I've no idea how adequate they are, but I think your great-aunt was careless about such matters. A lot of old people are. They were accustomed all their lives to being safe."

Emily thought fleetingly of the light in the upstairs

window. A burglar scared off by her ringing the doorbell?

"And now, Miss Armitage, if you'll just sign here. That's right, thank you. Well, good-bye. Mind how you go."

Mind how you go. A nice saying, but less innocent than it had once been. She was getting a little bored with familiar warnings. Nothing was going to happen to her between here and Bond Street.

But she would arrange for the new locks and bolts simply for Meggie's sake. Meggie wouldn't even have the advantage of hearing an intruder sneaking up on her.


She thought of the locks again when the very discreet young man at Cartier's looked at the emerald and diamond ring through a magnifying glass and said in an unmoved voice that its value was certainly not less than 6,000 pounds, probably more. It was a very fine emerald, almost flawless. He would take a measurement of Emily's finger, and give her a receipt for the ring. Perhaps she could call back the day after tomorrow. He was sure she would like to wear such a beautiful ring to the opera or the theater during her stay in London.

It was hardly the thing for a poor student, Emily thought. She was finding it difficult to remember that she was no longer poor. She would celebrate by taking some crumpets home for Meggie to toast for tea. She could walk from here to Hay Street, going down interesting side streets and into small alleys. London was a sort of rabbit warren above ground. Fascinating. Look at that small dark antique shop called Relics Ltd. The window crammed with rather dusty objects, and in the center—no, it just couldn't be—the gilt and enamel clock with the fat cherubs from Aunt Emilia's mantelpiece.

Emily was in the shop before she had stopped to think.

A bell clanged, and an elderly man with horn-rimmed glasses and a gray, neatly trimmed beard appeared behind the counter.

"The clock in the window—" Emily began.

"Yes?"

"It is for sale, isn't it?"

The man leaned forward to stare at her closely.

"Goodness me! You're extraordinarily like—" He seemed agitated and took off his glasses to polish them nervously. "No, I see now. I apologize. My eyesight isn't the best." The man put his glasses on again, and seemed to regain his composure. "It was a stupid mistake. Now, what was it you wanted to know about the clock?"

"First, where did you get it?"

"I'm afraid that isn't information I divulge, madam."

"Could there be two clocks like that?"

"Perhaps."

"But it is rare and old, so it isn't likely."

"My dear lady, in the antique world, anything is possible. The clock I am offering for sale is an original, but there could have been copies made at a later date."

"Yes," said Emily smoothly. "That's probably the explanation. I may have seen a copy. I'd know if I could look at it closer. Could I hear it chime? I'd recognize the chimes."

"I'm afraid it's out of repair, madam. It will need a considerable amount spent on it. I doubt if it would interest you."

"It would, you know," said Emily. "But if it is an original, I'll need some expert advice. I'll come back tomorrow."

"A good idea. One shouldn't buy objects of this quality on impulse."

"No. By the way, what is the price?"

The man hesitated, his eyes flickering behind the thick glasses. "We could discuss that when you return with your expert friend."

"I'd like to have some idea."

"Shall we say in the region of four figures? But we could come to an arrangement, perhaps."

Yes, perhaps we could. When I find out with certainty that that is Aunt Emilia's one and only eighteenth-century French clock, and how it got into the hands of this man.

Some girl who looks like me. . . . The voice that had said, "Emily Armitage speaking."

Shivery, eerie.

Who should she tell first, Patrick or Barnaby? Barnaby, of course. He had a good head on steady shoulders, Mr. Brinsley had said.


Meggie carried up the tea tray and put it beside the fire in the drawing room. The room was cozy, the curtains drawn, shutting out the growing dusk.

She was the girl upstairs now, Emily thought. She. No one else.

"What about your lunch?" Meggie asked in a voice that was just possibly intended to be solicitous.

"I had coffee and a sandwich," she said, enunciating slowly. "Sir Patrick is taking me out to dinner tonight."

Was there just a slight twinkle in the old woman's eye as she departed?

Emily got out the bundle of papers Mr. Brinsley had given her, and spread them out. Immediately she was lost in the fascinating world of her inheritance: Georgian silver, Waterford crystal, six small oil paintings (unidentified), Rockingham china, rare eighteenth-century Worcester vases, Chippendale furniture, Oriental rugs. Emily's eyes went up and down the columns, only taking in a detail here and there until she saw one eighteenth-century gilt and enamel French clock. So it had been here recently —broken by Meggie? Patrick? Barnaby? The girl who looked like her, whoever she was?

She told Barnaby about seeing the clock when she talked to him on the telephone a little later.

"Mr. Relics seemed a fishy character to me. First he seemed to think I had sold the clock to him, and then he had to change sides and treat me as a potential customer."

"Emily, my dear girl, how can you be so sure the clock was Mother's?"

"I can't. I just have this very strong hunch. It was so like the one I remembered. And this man wouldn't play the chimes. He said they were broken."

"Probably true."

"How do you explain it?"

"Suppose the clock was Mother's. Suppose she sold it some time before her death. This is probably just a case of one dealer selling to another. They're a species of cannibal, you know. Consume each other. But that's only guessing, and I'll certainly come with you tomor-

row and sort the mystery out. It's too late today. Mr.
Relics will be closed by now."

"Bless you, Barnaby, I knew you wouldn't laugh at
me. Naïve American let loose in London, slightly nutty."

"I'll laugh with you," said Barnaby in his serious voice.
"But Emily, love, don't get Mother's obsession for things."

"Good heavens, no! I couldn't be cluttered up like
that. I'm getting rid of everything except the things I
personally like."

"Such as?"

"Mainly that lovely diamond and emerald ring. I took
it to Cartier's today to have the fitting altered. They said
they'd do it at once."

"I can only say it will look marvelous on you. When
shall I come tomorrow? Can I take you to lunch? I'll
clear up my business appointments in the morning and
pick you up at one. Would you like to go to the Mirabelle?"

"Oh, Barnaby, Patrick's taking me there tonight."

"Is he?" Barnaby's voice remained equable. "Then
we'll go to Scott's."

"A sandwich in a pub near here would do, so we could
go to Mr. Relics' sooner."

"Mr. Relics will keep. By the way, don't let Patrick
take you gambling tonight. He used to do that with
Mother, with disastrous results."

"Is that why she had to sell the clock, do you think?"

"Not only the clock, I imagine."

"Well, I can sell a silver teaspoon, or something,"
Emily said blithely. "Anyway, who knows, I might be
lucky."

Barnaby was a nice, serious, reliable, darling man, and

she would gladly accept his advice on important matters. A night out with handsome Patrick didn't come under this heading. She intended to enjoy herself.

She put up her hair, stuck one of Aunt Emilia's topaz pins in its blonde swirl where it looked rather wonderful, took great care with some greenish eye shadow, and donned the chic new dress. Now if she didn't look her age, she looked at least three years older and appropriately sophisticated.

A Nefertiti neck, had she? Patrick certainly said original things.

It was five minutes to eight. She pulled the curtains back a fraction to look out. It was a little misty, but not too much to obscure the buildings opposite. The street was quiet, just one or two passersby. A girl coming into the telephone booth on the corner, an elderly gentleman walking a poodle.

In a minute she expected Patrick to come roaring up the street in his Jaguar or his Aston Martin.

A taxi trundled past and just afterward the girl emerged from the telephone booth. She paused and seemed to look up at the house, straight at Emily. She was tall and slender. Was her hair blonde? It was too dark to see. Yet Emily's heart was beating fast. She opened the window and craned out to see the girl walk swiftly away.

Who was she? The girl who had answered the telephone? Was she lurking to watch Emily go out, and then to get into the house again by her own private means?

Emily admonished herself. Was she going to get in a state every time she saw a slim blonde girl walking along a Mayfair street?

A few moments later Patrick's low red car swept up

and stopped outside her front door.

Emily ran down the stairs, suddenly extraordinarily glad to see him. She had the front door of the house open before he had finished locking the car.

"Hi!" she said, from the doorway.

"Emily! You look smashing."

"Oh, where have all the schoolgirls gone?" she chanted in a husky Dietrich voice.

"Fascinating," said Patrick. "How many people are you?"

"I'm only me, but I seriously think I may have a double. Never mind. Come on in for a drink."

"Scotch, please. What would you like to do this evening? Dinner, dancing, a drive down to look at the foggy Thames, tour the streets of Soho? Whatever."

"I'd like to do every one of those things, if there's time. Most of all, I'd like to walk around Mayfair. There's one shop in particular I want to look at again. An antique shop."

"Don't tell me you've caught Mother's collecting bug already?"

"Just something that intrigued me."

She would confront him with the clock, she had decided. If he were not prepared for its presence in Mr. Relics' window, he would respond naturally. And she would have a valuable second opinion before she confronted Mr. Relics with Barnaby tomorrow.

She wished she could stop thinking about the small, silly mystery of the clock.

"And what's this about your having a double?" Patrick said, accepted the Scotch and soda she had mixed him.

"Oh, nothing. I'll tell you later."

"No one," said Patrick soberly, "but no one could duplicate that lovely American nose."

"Let's talk about you," Emily said a couple of hours later, when coffee had arrived, and they were relatively alone in what must be a very privileged corner of a very beautiful restaurant. "We've covered cars, horses, the English climate, the best holiday resorts, a great deal of me, but nothing about Sir Patrick Lloyd, who has such influence with headwaiters."

She was thinking that lunching with Barnaby yesterday had been very pleasant, but she hadn't had this extreme curiosity to get inside his skull, because she had known more or less what she would find there. A good deal of honesty, kindness and caution. A very meritorious skull Barnaby would have. But what went on behind Patrick's long handsome face, with those narrowed, observant blue eyes, she really hadn't a clue.

He was very practiced at being a gracious host, and used to being with women, that was for sure. But she had this feeling that a sharp intelligence was at work behind the casual exterior. And it had nothing to do with taking attractive women out to dinner.

"Talk about me? Ah, now you have begun on an inexhaustible subject. My father was a country squire, lovable but completely idle. He dissipated the family fortune, and left my mother to pay for my upbringing. My mother, as you know, had me late in life when a baby was the last thing she wanted. Fortunately, she had inherited enough money from her previous husband, Barnaby's late father, to bring me up in the style such an exceptional infant deserved. Whether Barnaby resented this I will

never know. He's always far too polite to express thought
on the money I have had, which would have been his had
I not been born."

"Do you get on as brothers?"

"We don't seek each other's company."

"I'd gathered that. So what do you *do*, Patrick?"

"I enjoy good champagne. I like fast things—race
horses, cars, polo. Occasionally I like the gaming tables
at a good club. And I appreciate—with a connoisseur's
eye—pretty girls. Like you." He laid his hand over hers,
and Emily let it stay there, enjoying the contact. He had
nice hands. She could easily be attracted to him—was
already attracted.

"What else do you want to know?" he asked.

"What's under the charm? The real Patrick. Are you
idle like your father? Where do you get your money?"

"I'll tell you that when we're married."

"Patrick! Be serious."

He made a mock serious face.

"Well, shall we try our luck?"

"Luck?"

"At the tables? Oh, no, I forgot. You wanted to walk
through Mayfair. You said something about having a
double."

"I wasn't planning to look for her. I wanted to show
you something. Can we leave your car and walk?"

"Why not? We might just hear the nightingale in
Berkeley Square."

"I'm not that starry-eyed."

She could have sworn that she remembered the way.
Down Curzon Street, toward' Shepherd Market, round
a corner, up a little alleyway. There was the china and

pottery shop, the boutique, the coffee shop, the hat shop, and then—Surely this was where Relics Ltd. had been. Next to the hat shop. Surely. Yet here was a grocer's shop, the windows full of neat pyramids of canned food.

Then the antique shop was next to the grocer. But that proved to be a florist, the windows empty except for a few hardy potted plants.

Mr. Relics! Where, where, where was Mr. Relics?

"I must have come down the wrong street," Emily said. "I was absolutely certain this was where Mr. Relics was."

"Mr. *who?*"

"Mr. Relics. The shop was called Relics, and the man looked like one of them. You know, not certain which century he belonged to. I went in to ask about the clock."

"Emily, have I given you too much champagne?"

"You have not. My head is as clear as a frosty night. This . . ." Emily stabbed decisively at the pavement, "this is where Relics Ltd. should be. But it isn't," she added in bewilderment.

"My poor little muddled American, this was your first day in London."

"Which doesn't make me a half-wit." She shook her head. "He had this clock in the window that I am sure was Aunt Emilia's. When I inquired about it, first of all he thought I had brought it in—that's what I mean about having a double—but when he found I might be interested in buying it he just became a keen dealer. He wouldn't quote a price, and I wanted to bring Barnaby to see it, so I said we would call tomorrow. But now I've lost the shop."

"Let's look up his telephone number."

"What a good idea. There's a booth across the road."

By the light of the street lamp, Patrick scanned the list of R's.

"No," he said at last. "No Relics of any description. Sure you got the name right?"

"Of course I'm sure. I made a particular note of it."

"Well, a reputable antique dealer must have a telephone number. He would hardly be unlisted if he wanted to do any business."

"Then I'll just have to go on looking for the elusive Mr. Relics. I've turned a wrong corner, I expect. I don't suppose it will be the first time I get lost in London. But I'll find that shop if I wear my shoes out in the process."

"Let's go and get my car and drive around."

"All right," Emily agreed.

Past the luxurious shops, the narrow tidy doorways, the expensive gambling clubs, the restaurants with gaily striped awnings, the picture dealers, the gun shops, the small austere church, the ivy-covered walls and crumbling brick, the remains of ducal mansions and rich town houses. Up and down this much-lived-in part of the city, its tidy facade hiding its secrets.

Which facade hid Relics Ltd.? Because Emily was certain it was there somewhere. She simply hadn't dreamed it, even though Patrick was now suggesting that perhaps she had gotten confused and the shop was in Bloomsbury.

"It wasn't. It wasn't." Emily was trying not to be distraught. It seemed such a silly thing to get so upset about. "But never mind. I'll find it tomorrow, by daylight. I'm awfully tired now, Patrick. Can we go home?"

And that was the next strange thing. As Patrick drew up outside the house Patch was mewing reproachfully on the doorstep. He had somehow gotten shut out.

"Meggie must have opened the door for him to be out here," Emily said.

"You've had a caller," said Patrick. "I wonder who."

A caller? What was sinister about that? Why should the uneasiness stir in Emily again?

"Meggie is usually more careful about Patch, I must say," Patrick added. "She worships the monster."

"Then let's find out what it's about. Do you think Meggie will be very bad-tempered if we wake her?"

"Let me do it," Patrick said. "The old girl has a soft spot for me."

Meggie, wrapped in an ancient dressing gown, came grumbling up the stairs after Patrick. "Person can't get a proper sleep in this madhouse," she complained. "No, no one came here tonight," she said when asked.

"But Patch was on the doorstep, Meggie. How did he get out?"

"The bad boy! Was he then? How did he do that?"

"Did you open the door for any reason?" Patrick asked.

"Never had the need. Didn't hear no one."

"But Patch got out."

"Must have let him out when you went." Meggie looked at Emily as though she had been careless.

"No, Meggie. That didn't happen," Patrick denied. "Someone's been here. You didn't hear anything?"

"A burglar!" Emily said in alarm.

She was thinking of the girl she had seen emerge from the telephone booth, look up at the house, walk briskly away. The other Emily. . . . She, the house, was being watched.

"Well, come on, Emily. Let's go upstairs and count the silver."

Upstairs, Emily looked around the drawing room. It was too tidy for burglars, too tidy altogether. She crossed the passage to her bedroom and found the same scrupulous neatness, while Patrick went into Aunt Emilia's room.

Did he miss his mother? Had he loved her? Emily wondered. No doubt Aunt Emilia succumbed to his charm as well. But it would have been Barnaby to whom she had talked, upon whom she depended.

"Everything seems all right," said Patrick as Emily joined him in the big bedroom. "Funny. . . ."

"Funny, what?"

"Seem to smell something different. Not that ghastly attar of roses."

Was there the faintest smell of lemon, sharp, clinging? A younger person's perfume?

"It must be you," Patrick said. "Delicious, anyway."

"It was probably only Barnaby here, so there's nothing to be alarmed about, is there?" Emily said.

"Except what the devil would he be doing here?"

"He'll tell me tomorrow. Don't worry, Patrick. This is the first time I've ever seen you look serious."

"Hmm. I don't like being baffled. First Mr. Relics doing a Houdini trick, now Patch mysteriously outside."

"At least it wasn't you," Emily said, with a satisfaction that surprised her.

"Me? What do you mean?"

"Here tonight. With another girl."

Patrick laughed suddenly, and put his arm round her waist.

"No, you're my alibi, love. And I couldn't have a nicer one. Poor old Barnaby."

"Why poor old Barnaby?"

"He hasn't got an alibi. Has he?"

He hadn't. He merely said that he had spent the evening at home working on accounts, and had been asleep by midnight. His serious, sober gaze could not be challenged. Hadn't Emily, he said gently, become a little fanciful about the whole thing? The house, the imaginary light in the window. Patch shut out. Didn't all cats get accidently shut out once in a while? Patch, for all his bulk, could move with silent speed, and had surely escaped as Patrick and Emily had left for dinner. As for Mr. Relics, they would track down that shop after lunch. If it actually existed.

Oh, of course it existed, he added quickly, seeing Emily's indignation. But just where? After seeing Mr. Brinsley, she had walked from Theobald's Road, hadn't she? She must have passed countless alleys and small streets.

"Barnaby, I am absolutely certain that it was between Bond Street and Shepherd Market, because I saw it on my way from Cartier's."

She didn't add that she had, for an hour that morning, combed the narrow streets, though without success. It would make her story even more implausible.

The Atlantic flight, the time change, the excitement of her inheritance, her first visit to London alone, couldn't be constantly blamed for giving her hallucinations. She was a reasonable, level-headed person—always had been.

"Come now," Barnaby said. "Why don't you forget the whole thing? It probably wasn't Mother's clock you saw. Anyway, you couldn't prove Mr. Relics hadn't come by it legitimately."

Barnaby's eyes were so serious and gently reproving. "You really have got quite a lot already, Emily. Don't be greedy, like Mother was."

Emily nearly exploded.

"I'm *not* greedy. I'm only mystified. I don't like mysteries."

Then she was ashamed of herself.

"That," she said flatly, "was not the attitude Patrick took. He never accused me of greed."

"Neither am I. I'm just trying to point out the unimportance of the situation. You're going to get lost a thousand times in London over the next few weeks."

"I wasn't lost."

"Don't pout. Have a glass of wine."

They were having lunch at Scott's in Mount Street, but the atmosphere of luxury and the lavish food had no appeal today. Since arriving she had done nothing but eat expensive food. Barnaby and Patrick seemed to be trying to outdo one another in their efforts to impress her. That got wearing, and also a little puzzling. Neither of them, with their looks and obvious affluence, could be short of girl friends. Yet they had fallen on her, the little American cousin, as if she were manna from heaven.

Or someone to be watched, soothed, and kept out of mischief?

"Barnaby, I really want very little to eat. And I'm sure you have to get back to work."

"Miss Hopwood can cope. By the way, I want you to come back to my flat for tea, after we've established the existence of Mr. Relics."

"Now you're humoring me."

"Oh dear! How suspicious you are today. How are you getting along with old Meggie?"

"Fine. I'm getting to make her understand, but if she doesn't hear people in the house it's a bit of a problem."

"Seriously, Emily, no one could have gotten into the house, otherwise there would have been signs. Things disturbed."

"I admit I didn't have my fingerprinting equipment. But there was an atmosphere. Patrick felt it, too."

"Look, if you don't want to eat much, what about a nice salad? Then we'll carefully retrace your steps from Cartier's yesterday."

"Thank you, Barnaby. Sorry I got in a state."

"You're tired. Patrick kept you up late last night."

It was foolish to imagine that Barnaby could find a shop she couldn't find herself. It truly had vanished, and one might as well admit the fact.

"Okay, Barnaby. It must have been somewhere else that I saw it. But at least I now know this part of Mayfair by heart. And I'm suddenly feeling very English and longing for tea."

Barnaby's flat was exactly as she had imagined it, solid, dark, comfortable. She could hear someone moving about in another room.

"Who's that?"

"Miss Hopwood. I'll tell her she can go."

"You Englishmen with your faithful women—nannies, secretaries, housekeepers. You don't need wives, do you?"

They both laughed.

"And how are you planning to spend the evening?" Barnaby asked.

"Having an early night. I'm really tired. I'm going to stop turning things over in my head and go to sleep. Tomorrow I'll get properly unpacked and organized. I want to sort out all those things on the list Mr. Brinsley gave me. I have to decide what to sell and what to keep."

"If you want advice. . . ."

"I'll ask you immediately, I promise. But I want a day to browse by myself."

The evening passed peacefully. When the telephone rang, Emily approached it warily, and was relieved to hear Patrick's voice.

"Hi, Emily! Did you find your Mr. Relics?"

"No. I looked all morning, and this afternoon Barnaby came with me. It's the most mysterious thing. Barnaby is beginning to think I live in cloud cuckoo land."

"I was coming to town," Patrick said, "but one of my cows is sick."

"Cows? Now that's the best excuse ever. Do stay and hold its hand . . . hoof. Is it a special pet?"

"I'm afraid it's got mastitis—that's an inflamation of the udder, my city friend. I hope it isn't that, though. It would be disastrous for my herd."

"Herd! How many have you got?"

"Eighty Herefordshires at the last count."

"Oh! I didn't know you were being serious. I just never met a more unlikely person to be a farmer."

"I make a point of changing my boots before coming

to town," Patrick said. "When are you coming down to see my estate?"

"You didn't tell me you had one. You're supposed to be a young man about town."

"Barnaby's interpretation."

"Yes, it was." Emily was reflective. "I must say you put on a pretty good act, though."

"So does old Barnaby at being the proper gentleman."

"Is that an act? No, I don't believe you. You and Barnaby ought to be friends. For instance, why doesn't he know you raise cattle?"

"He knows I inherited a tumbledown manor house from my father, but I expect he thinks I use it for wild parties and a witches' coven. When are you coming down, Emily? Next weekend?"

"I don't know, Patrick. One old house is all I can cope with at present. I must get settled in."

"Okay. I understand. Mind how you go."

That injunction was being made a little too frequently. Was it significant? Or just English?


Mother seemed to think it significant when she called from Boston a little later.

"Emily, honey, are you all right?"

"I'm fine, Mother. What are you worrying about?"

"I just don't know. I guess I'm just fanciful. The other night you sounded funny."

"Did I? I didn't mean to. I'm fine, really. Patrick and Barnaby are wining and dining me, and I've seen Mr. Brinsley, the solicitor, who suggested putting what I didn't want in Sotheby's or Christie's auction rooms."

"Oh, I've heard of them. Which will you choose? You ought to go and watch a sale."

"What a good idea. I'll do that. Oh, and do you remember Aunt Emilia's diamond and emerald ring? It's heavenly, and I'm having it made to fit. I'm picking it up tomorrow—"

Although she had this intention, when she went to Cartier's the polite young man at the counter said the ring had already been collected. He frowned as he stared rather hard at Emily.

"Who collected it?"

"Miss Armitage."

"But *I am* Miss Armitage. What did this person look like?"

"Very like you, actually. Do you have a sister?"

"No, I do not. And I can't think how you could hand out a valuable ring to a stranger."

"I certainly didn't do that, Miss—er, Miss Armitage." The young man looked deeply affronted. "This person had our receipt."

"Show me."

"With pleasure. I assure you, we don't hand out pieces of jewelry irresponsibly."

The young man disappeared, to reappear presently with a receipt which certainly looked valid. It was a replica of the one Emily held herself. She opened her handbag to produce it triumphantly. She knew she had slipped it in the zipped pocket where she kept her traveler's checks. The traveler's checks were there. But the receipt from Cartier's was not.

It was no use to tip the contents of her handbag into her lap. The receipt was not there.

Emily thought frantically. When she had gone out to dinner with Patrick she had taken her evening bag, leaving this one behind in her bedroom. When Patch had been locked out by an intruder, naturally nothing had been disturbed in the house, for this scrap of paper was obviously all she, the intruder, had wanted. She? The girl in the telephone booth, of course. The girl who had collected the ring from this shop this morning. Was she working with Patrick? Had he taken Emily to dinner so the coast would be clear? Or was she, the look-alike, on Barnaby's team? Or alone?

"How long ago did this girl come in for my ring?" Emily asked.

"Shortly after we opened. We had to keep her waiting a few minutes."

Early, when she would have been certain Emily would not be about. "And did the ring fit her finger?"

"Yes it did—perfectly." The clerk clucked his teeth. "Miss Armitage, all this is most disturbing. I think you had better see the manager."

"No, I want to talk to my solicitor. Maybe the police. But I'll be back, you can depend on it." Emily stood up. "You won't disappear in the meantime, will you?"

"Disappear? Cartier's!" The young man's eyebrows shot up.

"I know. Worldwide reputation and all that. But people do disappear, and someone is fooling me. And it simply has to stop!"

She stood in the long dark hall of the mansion where Barnaby's flat was and kept her fi ger on the bell until the door was opened by Barnaby himself.

"Emily! What on earth are you doing here? You look upset."

"I am upset."

"Whatever has happened now? Come, wait in here." He steered her into a book-lined room. "I've got a client I must just get rid of. Won't be five minutes."

He closed the door, leaving her to study his taste in reading matter. She couldn't concentrate on the titles of the books, and failed to hear the front door shut as the client left. She hoped the excellent Miss Hopwood might be prevailed on to make some strong black coffee, but it appeared that she had not come in that day. Her mother was ill.

"So we're quite private," Barnaby said, when he returned to the library.

She rapidly related the Cartier episode, and had the satisfaction of seeing Barnaby's look of indulgence turn to concern and mystification.

"Well, I must say, it does seem as if you have a double."

"Who not only watches my house, but also has a key to it."

"Seems so." Barnaby stroked his chin.

"And Meggie is too deaf to hear her come in or leave. Or if she did happen to see her, she would think it was me. That's easily enough explained. What isn't explained is how she knows all my movements, like taking that ring to Cartier's."

"She must have just hit on the receipt in your handbag."

"The traveler's checks weren't touched."

"Too difficult to handle. This person would be a specialist in jewelry or antiques. Probably there's a gang."

"Mr. Relics!" Emily exclaimed.

"I don't know about him."

"But I do. He's disappeared because he's a receiver, what they call 'a fence' in our gangster films. He's probably played this trick dozens of times. And I think it's high time I went to the police. Will you come with me?"

"Of course. I'm afraid Cartier's won't care for it, you know."

"Well, that's their problem."

Barnaby smiled, rather stiffly.

"Perhaps you're right. But calm down and have some tea first. I've had a rough morning myself. Difficult clients. Can't pay their debts. Everyone has troubles."

The sergeant behind the desk in the small police station was courteous and attentive. He didn't seem in the least perplexed by Emily's bizarre story. Very bizarre things happened nowadays. He would come and have a look at the house. Perhaps she could tell him something about her late aunt's friends. Was there anyone to whom she may have given a key?

"Miss Armitage's great-aunt was my mother," Barnaby said. "And although I didn't know all her friends by any means, I know she had some slightly—well, eccentric ones. She met a lot of people everywhere—at her charity functions and in the gambling clubs with my brother."

The sergeant stared. "Did she win large sums of money? That would account for a break-in."

"No, she liked the glamour of it and only played for relatively small stakes. And she has been dead for six weeks, sergeant. These events have happened only in the last two days. Haven't they, Emily?"

The sergeant reflected. "In other words, after the arrival in London of the beneficiary. Could be someone had seen your mother wearing that valuable ring and knew Miss Armitage would be getting it out of the bank."

"Very plausible, sergeant."

"Someone has been watching the house," Emily said with conviction. "A girl who looks like me, talks like me."

"You've met the young lady?" the sergeant asked.

"No, but I've spoken to her on the phone. The night I arrived here. I was staying at the Connaught and I phoned my aunt's house. This girl answered. I'm sure it was she. But she hung up when she knew she'd made a mistake."

"Therefore she would have had to have access." The sergeant got ponderously to his feet. "We'd better go and take a look then."

The moment Emily turned the key in the lock the now familiar uneasiness swept over her. Don't be *silly*. There's nothing. Just an empty house, apart from Meggie and Patch in the basement. Just the usual quiet and solitude.

This time, however, the uneasiness was fully justified. Upstairs, the drawing room, full of its colorful clutter, had been ruined. Chairs were tipped over and their seats ripped out, drawers were lying upside down on the carpet, and more interestingly, a panel had been torn out of the wall beside the fireplace disclosing a small dusty aperture.

The sergeant put his hand in the opening.

"Seems to have been the late lady's wall safe. As you could say, the crux of the matter."

"What crux?" asked Barnaby tensely.

"Well, I work it out, from what Miss Armitage tells me about events, real or imaginary, there has been something in this house a thief was looking for. And he was running out of time, seeing as how you were planning to start selling things. Isn't that what you said, miss?"

"That's quite true."

"You wouldn't have any knowledge of the object he was looking for?"

"Not the faintest. Would you, Barnaby?"

"Afraid not. My mother was a great collector, sergeant, but an indiscriminate one. Some things were valuable, some not. And she liked hiding things. It was a sort of game she played." He regarded the aperture thoughtfully. "Whatever was in there must have been valuable, to be so carefully hidden. It also must have been something Mother didn't want to put in the bank. I didn't even know that secret panel existed. But old houses like this do sometimes have them. Our burglar obviously knew that. And this object won't be on Mr. Brinsley's list, if it was something Mother had kept quiet about."

"So we don't know what we're looking for. Makes the odds against catching our man a bit high." The sergeant shrugged. He seemed used to this kind of defeat. "I'll get the fingerprint boys over. Don't touch anything in the meantime. Is there anyone else in the house?"

"Only my old housekeeper in the basement," Emily said. "She's quite deaf."

"Get her up, please."

When Meggie saw the wreckage she gave a horrified cry, and pressed her hands to her face.

"Did you hear anything, madam?" shouted the sergeant.

"Only thought Miss Emily was bumping about a bit."

"But you saw nothing."

Meggie shook her head. "Not this time."

"You mean you have seen things on other occasions?"

Meggie shot Emily a veiled and resentful look. "Miss Emily does come in and out at all hours."

"But I don't, Meggie. I always tell you my plans."

Meggie didn't hear, or pretended not to hear, this protest. "Different when my lady was alive," she said sourly. "Never left Patch out."

"It's what I said, sergeant," Emily cried. "It's this girl who looks like me. She's either fooling Meggie, or Meggie *knows* what's happening."

The sergeant regarded Meggie thoughtfully, and only said, "Well, if she had poked her nose in this time, she'd probably have got herself knocked on the head."

"Them villains might have knocked me out," said Meggie, uncannily reading the sergeant's mind as she turned to go.

Emily had a wild thought and she put it into immediate operation. "Meggie!" she screamed at the retreating woman. "Watch out!"

Everyone jumped but Meggie.

It was hours before the police were gone, and Emily, with Meggie's help, had restored some sort of normality to the drawing room.

Barnaby had gone, too, though reluctantly. He didn't think Emily should be left only with a daft, deaf old woman whose honesty, he still felt, was in doubt. But Emily was insistent that she wasn't at all nervous. The worst had happened, hadn't it? A locksmith was coming to change the locks and after that she would be perfectly safe. She intended calling Mr. Brinsley and asking him if he had any idea what object Aunt Emilia could have hidden in that excellent hiding place. If he knew anything, she promised to inform both the police and Barnaby.

"Dear dear," came Mr. Brinsley's shocked voice. "Dear, dear, dear! Whatever this was should have been included in the valuation for death taxes. This is very irregular, indeed."

"But wouldn't you have known about Aunt Emilia's buying something so valuable? Wouldn't it have shown in her bank account?"

"That's the disturbing factor, Miss Armitage. Your aunt may possibly have had a considerable win at the gambling tables, and never have paid the cash into her bank account."

"Hidden it, you mean?"

"That, or the object she purchased with it."

"How much do you think it could have been, Mr. Brinsley?"

"I haven't the faintest idea. But I suppose it could have been . . . oh, I'd say maybe 10,000 pounds."

"As much as that?"

"Lady Lloyd wouldn't have thought much less than that worth hiding so carefully. I'm afraid she knew I didn't approve of her gambling habits, so she became very secretive. Why don't you ask your cousin, Sir Patrick, Miss Armitage?"

Did Patrick possibly know about that loose panel and the treasure trove behind it? She couldn't ask him because, unlike Barnaby, he hadn't given her his telephone number. Purposely?

Strangely enough, Emily slept soundly that night. Most likely it was because she had the feeling the intruder wouldn't be back. He, or she, had found the object of his search. First, there had been the clock, then the Cartier's receipt for the ring, then whatever was hidden behind that piece of paneling. The police had said that it wouldn't have taken an expert burglar more than ten minutes to locate that hiding place and to empty it quickly before Meggie was alarmed, or Emily came home.

The theft of the clock, and the jewelry receipt, had probably been the work of a woman. The police had interviewed the young man in Cartier's, and confirmed Emily's strange story that she had a double. They couldn't confirm the story about Mr. Relics of Relics Ltd. because, like everyone else, they had failed to trace that elusive establishment or its owner.

Emily guessed that Mr. Relics and the blonde girl had known Aunt Emilia and somehow learned her secrets.

But again one couldn't be entirely sure.

The next morning was glorious and Emily, waking refreshed and cheerful, decided she needed a brief escape from the bafflement of the last few days. She intended to be a tourist and simply sightsee—the Tate Gallery, the National Gallery, the famous auction rooms.

She wrote a note for Meggie, and was out of the house before even Barnaby, whom she was sure was an early riser, had had time to dial her number.

"Lot 74," the auctioneer on his rostrum intoned.

Emily looked at her catalogue. *Property of a Lady.*

DUTCH SCHOOL FLOWER SCENE, PAINTED ON PANEL, SIX INCHES BY EIGHT INCHES. EARLY FIFTEENTH CENTURY. ARTIST UNKNOWN.

A small, dark painting, unimpressive from this distance, but a marvel of delicate brushwork if one looked closely. Emily knew, because she had browsed about before the sale had begun. She loved early Dutch paintings. She would dearly have liked to buy this one, but the bidding was brisk and far beyond her pocket.

"Who will offer me three thousand pounds? Three thousand five hundred. Four thousand. Four thousand five hundred. Five thousand. Five thousand I am bid. Five thousand two hundred. The bidding is against you, sir. Five thousand three hundred; five thousand five hundred. Five thousand five hundred I am bid. Any advance on five thousand five hundred? Going, going, gone. . . ."

The hammer tapped smartly, and there was a stir in the crowd as two people prepared to leave before the next picture was offered. A man and a girl. They were smiling at one another with obvious satisfaction. Emily distinctly heard the girl say, "That's a thousand more than you expected. Pleased?"

For his answer the man took her arm and squeezed it. He wasn't wearing his thick glasses, and his neat little gray beard had gone, but Emily had an excellent memory for faces. She would have known Mr. Relics anywhere.

She wouldn't have known the blonde girl because she had never met her face to face. And today her hair was tied back in a neat ponytail instead of hanging loose, the way Emily wore her own. She couldn't alter the shape of her face, however, or the color of her wide blue eyes. She did bear a remarkable resemblance to Emily, there was no doubt about it. Even the careful young man in Cartier's had every excuse for being fooled.

Her heart thudding with excitement, covering her face with her catalogue, Emily sprang up to follow the two. A group of people blocking the doorway halted her. By the time she had edged through, the stairway was empty. She flew down it, and out into the street, just in time to see the girl, followed by Mr. Relics, get into a taxi and drive off.

Now she had lost them!

But what could she have done, anyway? She couldn't have accosted them and accused them of theft. Those things had to be proved; it was a matter for the police.

But the nice sergeant would be deeply interested in her discovery. So would Barnaby. She must rush home and telephone them both.

*Property of a Lady.* . . . It would not be difficult to find out who had put that picture in the sale. Then surely the rest would be simple.

Provided, of course, it had been stolen from Aunt Emilia. Not from the hiding place behind the paneling, because it must have been in Sotheby's some time, waiting for today's sale. Perhaps at the same time the little gilt clock had disappeared. No, before Aunt Emilia's death, since it did not appear on the lists. Aunt Emilia must have been being slowly drained of her more valuable possessions while she lay ill.

Patrick's red Aston Martin stood outside her door, and in the drawing room Patrick's long body rose out of a low chair.

"Surprise," he said. "Hope I'm welcome."

"Oh, yes, of course you are. How are the livestock?"

"Doing better, thank you. I've an exceptionally good vet."

Emily shook her head and smiled in disbelief.

"What's the matter?"

"I really can't believe it."

"Believe what?"

"You . . . a farmer."

He smiled back. "Those are the facts. But seriously, I love it and I don't know why it surprises everyone. And I'm good at it. Since I've put my hand to the plow, as they say, I've long ago paid off all my youthful gambling debts —oh, yes, I promised that none of my inheritance nor any of Mother's money would go for that. Don't you know that's one of the reasons Mother left you the house? It was to make a man of me," he teased. "I don't really mean that, but she saw that I was doing well on my own and she wanted it to stay that way. I no longer gambled heavily and I was becoming a responsible subject of the crown."

"But Barnaby?"

"Oh, old Barnaby's got his feet squarely on the earth and, truthfully, I think Mother felt he wouldn't know how to enjoy it. But you—you poor little far-off American waif—you would suddenly be an heiress, something of which you'd never even dreamed, a Cinderella. Well, Mother was like that, full of sudden surprises. Do you know she once washed her hair in champagne at a garden party because the Prince of Wales dared her to do so? And once she died it pale green to match a dress."

Emily laughed. "She didn't?"

"So help me." All at once he stopped and took her

in. "I say, you *are* a pretty girl. You look a lot like the photographs of Mother at your age." He stood tall above her. "I am going to do something," he said, his mouth curving softly. "I am going to kiss you." He put his hands on her shoulders and brought her to him.

His kiss was gentle and he smelled of the outdoors and sun and new grass. She felt her own lips yielding, but she drew gently away. "Not now, Patrick. Not now, please."

Was he deceiving her? Was he winning her over with his irresistible charm only because he was the one involved with her look-alike? Was Patrick the thief? She wouldn't blame him, even though what he had told her had the sound of truth.

A look of skepticism crossed her face.

"I get it," he said, shaking his head in several quick, understanding nods. "I'm still number one on the list of suspects—Patrick, the wastrel; Patrick, the gambler; Patrick, the playboy."

"Oh, Patrick, I didn't mean to. . . ."

"Of course, you did. And why shouldn't you? I *do* like to gamble . . . I *do* like fast sports cars . . . I *do* like to have a good time . . . I *do* like pretty girls. Whatever that makes me, it doesn't make me a thief."

Emily buried her face in her hands. "Oh, Patrick, I don't know what to think any more. I am so confused and bewildered. I want so much to believe you."

"Then do so."

"Will you help me?"

"Of course, I'll help you."

She took his hands in hers. "I saw the girl today . . .

the girl who looks like me. And who do you think she was with? Mr. Relics!"

"Are you sure?"

"Positive. They were in Sotheby's. They had just made a rather profitable sale of a small Dutch painting. About so big." She held out her hands. "Dark. A flower scene. *Property of a Lady*. Do you remember it?"

"No. Should I?"

"If it were your mother's, yes."

"You think they are stealing Mother's things and selling them?"

"Yes, I do. It's much more than the little clock. There was the burglary yesterday, and that lovely ring disappeared from Cartier's. . . . But you don't know about that."

"What do you want me to do to help?"

"Come with me to Mr. Relics' shop," she said.

"But you can't even find it." He took her shoulders again. "Emily, darling, give up on that one. You must have dreamed it. You were exhausted and upset. There's no such person as Mr. Relics."

Distrust flickered in her eyes. He spotted it and removed his hands from her shoulders.

"Be patient with me," she said. "I think I can find Mr. Relics' shop. At least I think I have a hunch."

"Okay, okay. I'll come along with you. But fill me in about this burglary and the missing ring."

She felt his eyes upon her, wondering, searching, trying to read in her face whether or not she was truly mad. After all, shops did not normally disappear like mirages . . . even to the British, who believed in ghosts.

"There!" said Emily, standing in front of a small shop, the window of which was full of canned foods in neat pyramids. The door was locked, not surprisingly since it was after closing time. The shops on either side were closed, too, which was unfortunate, for otherwise their occupants might have told an interesting story about their neighbor who had changed from antiques to groceries —nonperishable—overnight.

"I'm sure this was Relics Ltd.," Emily said with deep conviction. "I could swear there was that hat shop on one side. And I remember the hollows in the steps."

"Most old stone steps have become hollowed over the centuries."

"I just know these," Emily insisted. "I'm sure Mr. Relics and that girl are hiding behind those cans of beans."

"Shall we knock?"

"No. What could we do except frighten them off? Let's go home and I'll call my nice sergeant."

"Will he believe you?"

"I think so. He has so far, and I've told him some odd things."

"Like me, he's probably just a sucker for a pretty face."

"Nothing of the kind. He certainly won't be when I tell him about Sotheby's today."

The sergeant, however, although attentive to Emily's story, was guarded. He said he would send a man round to the shop in question, but if no one could be roused she was to understand there could be no breaking in on such slender evidence. No evidence at all, really. English law didn't operate on hunches. But the premises could be kept under observation if his man reported that he shared any of Emily's suspicions.

He warned her to keep silent about it, however. Didn't want the culprits scared off.

"Who shouldn't I talk to?" she demanded.

"Nobody. Your cousins. That old Welsh woman."

"My cousins! You can't mean that, sergeant."

"I mean what I say, ma'am."

"Rubbish!" exclaimed Patrick. "Not talk to me? Anyway, it's too late. You have."

Emily nodded. "And that's why I think it only fair to talk to Barnaby, too."

"Now?"

"Now."

"You're going to telephone?"

"No, I'm going to stand on his doorstep. You don't have to come."

"Do you want me to?"

She looked at him pleadingly. "Yes."

"Good. Let's go."

Disappointingly, it seemed as if their journey would be as fruitless as the one they had made to the small innocent-looking shop with its windowful of groceries. They stood outside Barnaby's solid mahogany door and rang the bell again.

"Do you know Miss Hopwood, Barnaby's secretary?" Emily asked.

"No, thank goodness. Do you?"

"No. She was away the other day when I was here. Had a sick mother."

"Not a deceased grandmother?"

"What do you mean?"

"Time off for Granny's funeral. A stock English joke."

"You think her mother wasn't sick at all?"

"If she has a mother."

Before Emily could answer that cynical and surely unwarranted conjecture, a door at the end of the corridor opened. A woman with a Pekingese on a leash emerged.

"No use your ringing Mr. Chisholm's bell, darlings," she said. "He went out half an hour ago."

"Oh, too bad," said Patrick.

"If it's important, I know they often go to the Camellia for dinner. It's just around the corner, to the right. Pretty little place, but most overpriced."

"*They?*" Emily and Patrick asked in unison.

The elevator came.

"Yes. Mr. Chisholm and that pretty little secretary of his—she's a lot like you," the woman said to Emily. "In you go, Pookie."

"Miss Hopwood?" Emily asked.

"I don't know her name. I'm not a nosy neighbor. Mind my own affairs, I do."

"Of which I'd say she's had a few," Patrick whispered as the woman exited before them.

"I am thoroughly confused," Emily said as he took her arm and led her down the street. "I was under the impression Barnaby had Miss Hopwood for years."

"So was I," said Patrick. "Well, we'll soon have the answer to it all. Onward, my dear, to the Camellia."


"It's too dark," Patrick said as they entered. "I always distrust dark restaurants. I suspect they're trying to hide the food. Still . . . this is a marvelous place for a rendezvous—all this pink light and foliage."

"Barnaby? A rendezvous? A tryst?"

"Why not? Particularly if this Miss Hopsack. . . ."

"Hopwood," Emily corrected.

"Particularly if this Miss Hopwood—if indeed she *is* Miss Hopwood—looks as much like you as I suspect she will."

"Oh, Patrick . . . I don't like it. I just can't. . . ."

"Two, sir?" said the headwaiter, materializing from behind a large potted palm.

"Please," said Patrick.

"Could we have that table in the little alcove . . . over there in the corner?" Emily suggested. "It looks so cozy."

"Clever girl," Patrick whispered, for the table had a clear view of the whole room, an excellent vantage point.

The headwaiter ushered them to the table Emily had requested and seated them within the niche which was flanked by two lovely palms and adorned with hanging ferns.

"Something to drink, sir?" he asked.

"By all means," Patrick answered. He scanned the room once the waiter had taken the order and shook his head. "No Barnaby, I'm afraid."

Emily pressed his hand in warning. "Don't look now, but two tables away on our right. . . ."

"Who?" Patrick said, having swung around immediately to stare at the couple, a fair-haired girl with her back to him and an elderly man wearing horn-rimmed glasses, drinking champagne.

"Mr. Relics," Emily said. "And his accomplice. What a coincidence."

"Excuse me a minute, my dear." Patrick sprang up and crossed to the other table, holding out his hand and exclaiming, "Emily Armitage! Cousin Emily, by all that's wonderful. When did you arrive in London? Why didn't you tell me you were coming? Have you seen Barnaby? Don't tell me you've been calling on him and not on me. This is his patch of London, isn't it?"

The gray-haired man had pushed back his chair. His eyes were glittering with some emotion that looked very much like panic.

"You're making a mistake, sir. This lady is not your cousin."

"But how can you know, since you don't know who I am?" Patrick said.

The girl had gone pale. Her wide eyes were fixed on Patrick. They also showed panic. "Nor do I know who you are. I've never seen you before."

"But I'm Patrick, darling. Won't you introduce me to your friend? Oh, I say, have I really made a mistake? Am I interrupting a celebration?"

"Yes, you are," the man exclaimed.

"And I see you're expecting another guest." Patrick indicated the third place laid at the table. "I *do* apologize. I could have sworn you were Emily," he said to the girl. "Extraordinary likeness. Except for your voice. If you hadn't opened your mouth I would have sworn you were my cousin. So sorry."

He returned to his own table. Emily had had the sense to take out a mirror and attend to her face, screening it from view.

"Well?" she whispered, kicking Patrick under the table. "What's she like?"

"She's a hard, calculating little witch. Eyes like ice. Am I right in guessing Mr. Relics is calling for the bill?"

"No," said Emily slowly. "No, because here comes Barnaby."

Patrick nodded. "Thought he'd show up. Someone is going to sit at that third place and pay for the champagne. Don't go on hiding behind that mirror, darling. Let everyone see you."

Emily lowered the mirror, raised her eyes and found herself staring straight into Barnaby's face.

"Emily! Patrick! I heard you were looking for me. Has something more happened? I hope not."

"Can't we meet your friends?" Patrick said.

"What friends?" Barnaby's face went blank.

"Miss Hopwood, I presume," Emily said.

"Miss Hopwood? Miss Hopwood's home. I've just deposited her at her flat. She's very upset about her mother. On my way back I ran into Mrs. Colton, my neighbor. She said you were looking for me and that she had sent you here."

Emily and Patrick looked at each other.

"All right," Barnaby said. "I guess I have some explaining to do." He sat down heavily in one of the two vacant chairs.

Patrick kept a sharp eye on Mr. Relics and Emily's double. Since she was not Miss Hopwood, they couldn't lose her—or Mr. Relics.

"I suppose the cat's out of the bag, somehow," Barnaby said. "I mean, you two obviously know about me and Miss Hopwood . . . Helen and me."

"Know what?" Patrick asked.

"That we're going to be married." He looked at their puzzled faces.

"Oh, Barnaby, no!" Emily said.

"Why not?" Barnaby answered. "She's a very nice young woman."

"*Young* woman? I thought Miss Hopwood was old . . . I mean you've had her for years," Patrick said.

"No, no. That was Helen's aunt, Audrey Hopwood. She's been gone for nearly a year. Helen's quite young, nearly ten years younger than I."

Emily laughed. "And I thought you were courting me."

"I was, sort of," Barnaby said. "At least I was testing . . . if you'll forgive me. I wanted to make sure about Helen."

"And I flunked out," Emily said with a wide smile. "Now you're sure."

"Not at all," Barnaby said. "You were so charming, so appealing I thought I'd better ask Helen quickly. So I did, and we're going to be married next month."

Emily said to Patrick, "What are our friends at the next table up to?"

"Talking," Patrick said. "And I think trying very hard to remain collected. They don't know quite what to do."

"What on earth are you two talking about?" Barnaby asked.

"We are. . . ." Patrick stopped cold at the sight of a new arrival.

Barnaby followed Patrick's glance. "I say," he said, "isn't that Mother's solicitor, Mr. Brinsley?"

"It most certainly is," said Emily.

"Don't let him see you," Patrick said.

"Why not?" asked Emily.

"Because I think he's going to join your Mr. Relics and your double. Quick! Put up your menus. You, too,

Barnaby. If he sees us, it will scare him off."

"What *is* going on?" Barnaby asked.

"We'll explain later, Barnaby, but for now please do as I say."

"Mr. Brinsley? I can't believe it." Emily was astounded. "That character out of Dickens, that sweet old man."

"Don't forget Dickens created some sharpies, as well —Fagin, Bill Sykes," Patrick pointed out. "Barnaby, do you think you can slip behind those potted plants without being seen and get a policeman? Hold him at the front entrance and I'll drive our trio right into the net."

"Too late," Emily said. "Mr. Relics has just made for the door."

"Don't worry about him," Patrick said. "He'll head back to his hideaway at his now-you-see-it, now-you-don't shop, and our waiting policeman will grab him. Okay, Barnaby, they're not looking now."

Barnaby still looked bewildered but he said, "All right," and slipped off his chair and behind a plant.

"What do you think they'll do?" Emily asked. "Obviously Mr. Relics has told Brinsley we're sitting here."

"I'm not so sure. They seem to be in a quandary about how to play their big scene, I'd say. Brinsley! It's incredible!"

"How's Barnaby doing?" Emily inquired from behind her menu.

"Pretty good so far. Oh, oh. The headwaiter has spotted him."

"Mr. Chisholm, is anything wrong?" the headwaiter asked, as Barnaby hid behind a huge palm.

"I am going to know this menu by heart," Emily said. "Has Brinsley seen Barnaby?"

"I don't think so. Old Barnaby's staying crouched and . . . well, *well*, I didn't know the old boy had it in him. He's clutching his stomach and staying low, as though he had violent cramps. Marvelous! He's kept his face hidden and now he's off and away!"

"I feel so ashamed, thinking it was Barnaby."

"Why? You thought I was the culprit for a while as well. But never mind that. I think it's time to make our move on Mr. Brinsley."

They got up together and headed toward the other table.

"The voice," Emily said. "She must have gotten that from those tapes Mother and I sent to Aunt Emilia. . . . And she must have been expecting Mr. Brinsley or Mr. Relics to call the night she answered the phone."

"You've just passed your Criminology final exam," Patrick said, widening his smile as they approached.

Brinsley turned ashen, at the sight of them, and Miss Look-Alike flushed violently.

Brinsley's head dropped into his hands as Patrick and Emily seated themselves at the table.

"Well," said Patrick, "as the elephant said, we're all ears."

Mr. Brinsley looked up and spread out his hands.

"I suppose it all started one night when your mother, Lady Lloyd, had made a huge win at the tables. I was in the club later that evening—yes, you can raise your eyebrows—but I rather enjoy games of chance and I had overindulged myself. This night, when I went in, everyone was talking about Lady Lloyd's fantastic win. And yet she made no mention of that money to me, her solicitor. Naturally, I thought it must be in the house."

"And was it?" Patrick asked.

"We couldn't find it."

"Don't implicate me in this, you old fool," his blonde companion said.

"Old fool is it now? Well you, my young fool, are in this up to your pretty little ears."

She made a gesture toward moving, but Patrick's strong hand restrained her. "Not so fast, my dear. I think you'd better just sit tight."

How could anyone think she really looked like Emily with those cold, cold eyes?

"What did you think happened to the money?" Patrick asked.

"You knew your mother better than I. Some whim made her hide it—like the preservation of English walnuts. She drove me crazy with her ridiculous charities and absurdities. When the time came, I felt I was entitled to more."

He spread his hands again. "Unfortunately, I was able to remove only a few select items from the house while she was ill. Then she died, and the house was sealed tight until the government's tax man could be there for the appraisal and listing of goods. That left me only the money to search for, but I had no luck. Then you arrived, and when you said you would be selling some of the furniture, I had to move fast. You'd probably sell the very piece in which she'd hidden the money."

"And, of course, it was you who suggested I take my ring to Cartier's and leave it for cleaning and adjustment," Emily said. She found she could not look at her double. Instead, she gestured at the girl with the cold eyes and said, "And how did she come into this?"

Mr. Brinsley actually beamed. "It was pure luck," he said with pride. "I was in despair over ever finding the money and my debtors were pressing me. Then by chance I met Sandra. She looked so like the photographs your aunt had of you that the situation cried out to be exploited. I knew she could learn to impersonate you and that once you were here, she could dispose of valuables—or claim them, as she proved with the ring—as easily as you."

There was a tapping on the window from outside and Barnaby, looking very Scotland Yard, motioned that he had a policeman at the front entrance.

"Shall we?" said Patrick, rising to his feet, and putting a bill on the table. "I must say I won't forget this place in a hurry." He looked curiously at Brinsley. "What ever made you choose it? Isn't it a bit out of the way?"

"Well, yes," Brinsley said. "But someone told me it was secluded and had excellent—" He stopped and a peculiar look of dismay came over his face. "I just recalled who it was that recommended it," he said haltingly. "It was that young pup—"

"Barnaby?" Patrick broke in. "Ah, yes, tripped up by your subconscious. I rather like that."

Out in the cold night air, Emily took a deep breath. "Oh, how I'd like to be there when Mr. Relics walks right into the police! I'm not a vindictive person, but. . . ."

"Look," Patrick said, "let's go round with Barnaby and the others and sort this all out for the sergeant and tomorrow . . . tomorrow we'll go to my place in the country. You'll love it, darling. It's green and peaceful and the air is like pale, dry wine. . . ."

"Patrick?"

"Yes."

"There's still a bit of unfinished business."

"What's that?"

She stood on tiptoes and offered her lips. "As I was saying before we were so rudely interrupted. . . ."

He smiled down on her. "You Americans," he said, "are a very remarkable people."

"And you British," she said, "certainly have a way with mysteries."

"There's no mystery about this," he said, then kissed her. "You know, for all of her madcap life, Mother made some really marvelous decisions."

A bobby rounded the corner. "Good evening," he said. "Lovely night."

"Magnificent night," Emily said, hooking her arm through Patrick's. "Just about the most beautiful night I can ever remember."

The bobby smiled. "Mind how you go," he said.

# The Lady and the Tycoon

Eileen stood in the bare room feeling both exultant and
sad. An empty house was always sad. Until one had
redressed it and made it one's own it belonged to its
ghosts.

This old house, a little neglected but structurally sound,
was a singularly lucky find. It was exactly what she had
been looking for, and at the right price, for it was too far
from a town and a railway station for competitive bidding. Neither of these things mattered to Eileen. The
house was in the country and Peter could ride a bicycle
to school. Her remaining capital would be just enough
for them to live on. Perhaps later she could sell flowers
or fruit. There was a large garden.

Her reflections were broken as Peter came bursting in. "I say, Mum, there's an enormous Rolls at the front gate, with a chauffeur. Someone's coming in."

Eileen heard the footsteps on the gravel path and the clang of the door knocker. "It can't be anyone for us. We've only owned the house for an hour. Go and see who it is, Peter."

Almost at once the man was in the room. He hadn't even waited for Peter to announce him. "Mrs. Fairley, my name's Heseltine. I believe you've just bought this house."

"Yes, I have."

"I'll offer you another thousand to sell."

"You'll—what?"

She stared at him, noticing his beautiful clothes, his black glossy hair, his hands, soft and well-kept but shaped like a workman's. A hard jaw. Dark, impatient eyes.

But her impression of his physical appearance was vague. What obsessed her was resentment at his arrogance. "Mr. Heseltine, I have just bought this house. Why should you assume that I immediately want to sell it?"

"I'm offering you a handsome profit."

"But I didn't buy it to make a profit. I bought it to live in. My son and I are going to live here." She spoke slowly and carefully, as if this stranger, in his impatience, might not be able to take in such a simple explanation.

"Fifteen hundred."

"I beg your pardon! Look, I'm afraid you don't understand. The auction is over. The house is mine."

The man smiled suddenly. The smile was like a light in his dark face; a light turned on by a switch being pressed; part of his stock in trade, like his Rolls and his checkbook. "I know the sale is over," he said. "Unfortunately I cut it a bit fine and got caught in an infernal traffic jam. Otherwise I'd have been there and got the house. Since I wasn't, I'm asking you to resell to me at a considerable profit."

"Do you always get what you want, Mr. Heseltine?"

"Always."

Eileen walked across the empty room to the bow window that looked out over the tangled garden. There was a copper beech, a pair of elms at the gate. A bird bath, a sundial, roses growing over a trellis, crazy paving. The grass needed cutting. The garden was full of weeds. She would be happily busy for months. "Not always, Mr. Heseltine," she said abstractedly. "Not this time."

He took a step towards her. His gaze took in her good but shabby tweed suit, her tawny hair done in a simple style that allowed her to avoid the expense of hairdressers. Being obviously a rich man, he read her financial position immediately. Her emotions were another thing. He wouldn't have thought them important. "Come, Mrs. Fairley. Don't be too hasty. You could send that nice-looking lad of yours to a good school if you accept my offer."

"Perhaps I could. But I happen to think a home is more important. We haven't had one, not a real one, since his father died." She touched the windowsill lovingly. "Now we have."

"You mean you're absolutely refusing my offer?"

"Absolutely."

"Do you know who I am?"

"You said your name was Heseltine."

"Gordon Heseltine."

"Of course! The property tycoon. Then why are you interested in an old house like this right in the country?"

"Never mind why I want it. I do want it. I usually get what I want."

"Yes. You told me that before. I'm so sorry. You've had a journey for nothing. And I can't even offer you any refreshment. I'm really so sorry."

"Will you and the boy come and have dinner with me in Tradminster?"

Humour glinted in Eileen's eyes. "Good gracious, Mr. Heseltine, you won't get round me that way."

"Then I shall have to find another way."

He was staring at her with his remarkably penetrating gaze. She felt a prickle of uneasiness. She didn't like the soft thoughtfulness of his voice. A man like him would have plenty of methods of getting his own way. She had read of his property deals. If he wanted the Tower of London he would no doubt eventually get it. Who was she, one financially insecure woman, to stand against him? Her chin went up. "I'm sure your time is valuable, Mr. Heseltine. I wouldn't waste any more of it if I were you."

He went as he had come, abruptly, not saying goodbye. This, she realized, was not deliberate bad manners but a preoccupation with his new, small, irritating, unexpected problem.

Involuntarily she smiled. She felt she had managed to stand upright against a hurricane. And would continue to do so. The house was hers. She and Peter had a home. She could not be cajoled, bribed or threatened into selling.

Peter came rushing in. "Mum, do you know, that man was a millionaire. The chauffeur told me."

"Yes, I know."

"What did he want?"

"He was rather annoyed because he had missed buying this house. But we had got in first. Now we'd better go if we want to get back to the village before dark."

"Mum, will you buy my new bike tomorrow?"

"Perhaps." Her glance went round the dusk-filled room. "We'll need a million things. Peter, are you disappointed you're not going to boarding school?"

"Well, I——" He was a sensitive child, her son. He didn't quite meet her eyes. "Not if I have a new bike," he said.

They settled in slowly. Eileen decided, not without pleasure, that there would still be things needed when Peter was a grown man. She liked planning and looking ahead. The green carpet from the London flat would do for this year. Curtains and a new refrigerator must come first. The furniture looked sparse in the big rooms. One day she would get two more armchairs, perhaps a painting to hang over that lovely fireplace.

Gordon Heseltine would have done everything in a day. What a lot of fun he would have missed, such as working in the garden and discovering unsuspected small tender plants among the rioting goldenrod and michaelmas daisies. He would have had an army of workmen and given his terse orders. Eileen smiled, thinking of the unaccustomed frustration he must be suffering. But what could a man like that, who could buy a fifty-bedroomed mansion or a penthouse, want with this rather small house set in fields in the middle of nowhere?

She thought she had forgotten him, but then he appeared again, and his square-jawed face with its level brow and keen gaze was so familiar that she wondered how it had slipped out of her mind at all. Her heart was thudding uncomfortably as she took him into the drawing room. She hadn't quite enough courage to keep him standing on the doorstep. In any case he seemed to be in an affable, unthreatening mood. He said it had interested him to call and see how she had settled down. His voice was soft and deep and pleasant. It didn't lull her into any feeling of security, but involuntarily it made her offer him a glass of sherry, which he accepted.

"So you have no designs on my house today?"

"None at all." He looked round the room approvingly. "I like what you've done."

"Everything's rather shabby, I'm afraid."

"It fits. You wouldn't want new things in a room like this." He really seemed to like the faded chintzes. But his gaze kept coming back to her as if she were part of the decoration scheme.

"Mr. Heseltine," she said uneasily, "you haven't come just to admire my furniture. What is it?"

"Well, as to that, I thought it only courtesy to tell you. I've bought the fields surrounding this place. Ten acres. I'm planning a housing estate. Small houses for workers. Preferably people with children." He gave his sudden illuminating smile. "You may think of me as just another man out to make money, but that isn't the entire truth."

Eileen seldom lost her temper. She didn't know why she did so now, except that in the middle of what she had imagined to be an amnesty he had struck her down. "Spare me the hypocrisy, Mr. Heseltine," she exclaimed.

"Since when has a man of your kind ever thought of a worker as a human being? This is merely a way of driving me out of this house, isn't it?"

He smiled again, his gaze uncomfortably penetrating. "Since you put it bluntly, yes."

"But *why*? Peter and I are happy here. Why must you come, like a bulldozer——" She went to the window to look out at the green fields, the precious quiet fields that framed the old house. "This is a rural area. The council won't give you planning permission."

"Won't they?"

She looked at him hopelessly, knowing already his methods. What small country councillor would stand against a man of his wealth? "You know a housing estate such as you describe would ruin this perfect house."

"I know."

"But if you were to own it, what then?"

"I would use the fields for my horses."

"You really mean this, don't you?"

"Oh, I mean it, Mrs. Fairley." His voice was soft, beguiling. "Pay me the compliment of overestimating, not underestimating, me." He was about to go. He turned back as an afterthought. "My original offer to you still stands. And by the way, I stopped and took a look at the school your boy's going to. It's not good enough for a lad like that. Believe me."

"Peter dear——" It was late and her conscientious son was still poring over his homework. "You do like this school . . . ?"

"It's all right."

"But it's not boarding school, is that it?"

Peter kept his eyes on his work. He was too young for such self-possession. "I said it's all right."

"Daddy said I was always to provide you with a home. I have, haven't I?" He nodded, switching back the lock of hair that always fell in his eyes.

"But I suppose it can be a home wherever it is. A flat in London, for instance. I expect you'd be happy enough there if it were only for school holidays. I could get a job."

She was thinking aloud, not realizing at once the blazing excitement in his lifted eyes. "Mum, you mean I could go to boarding school then? Would we be able to afford it?"

"With Mr. Heseltine's help, yes."

"Mr. Heseltine? Did he come again?"

Eileen smiled wryly. "He thought we might be getting a little lonely out here. He was planning to surround us with about a hundred families. I'd have gladly put up with that to spite him. But he seems to know more about my own son than I do." Her eyes darkened with anger. "Why didn't you tell me how much you wanted to go to boarding school?"

"Oh, well, Mum, Mr. Heseltine is a man. He understands."

So not only did she have to let Mr. Heseltine win, but she had to submit to the galling knowledge that Peter thought him a paragon. Very well, she would go down fighting. She wrote the briefest of letters to Mr. Heseltine saying that if he raised his offer by five hundred pounds she would be prepared to consider it. Would he please address correspondence to her solicitor?

She could hardly bear to pack the possessions she had so lovingly arranged about the house. All the same, now it had come to it, she couldn't get away quickly enough, not only because she was already imagining Gordon Heseltine striding about the rooms giving his imperative orders, but because she was so ashamed of herself. She had imagined her own happiness living quietly in the country would also be Peter's. She hadn't tried to discover his feelings. It had taken a stranger whom she thoroughly abhorred to show her this. She hoped passionately that she would never need to encounter Gordon Heseltine again.

It didn't seem that she would. The business was transacted through her solicitor. It was true that Mr. Heseltine sent a message saying that if she had difficulty in finding a flat in London, or if she would like any help in deciding on a good preparatory school, she must not hesitate to get in touch. "Seems a decent chap for one of his kind," said her solicitor.

"Yes. Now he's got his own way. That's just a small bonus for the victim."

So she was back in London, a bachelor girl, going to work each morning as a receptionist in a private hotel, and returning at night to the neat small maisonette in St. John's Wood.

She renewed acquaintance with her old friends simply because she was so lonely. She went to several of their parties. It was at one of these that she met Mark Denning. He was a scientist employed in the laboratory of one of the big chemical groups. He was slight and diffident and, from the moment of their meeting, full of admiration for her. The admiration overcame the diffidence, and before long they were dining together and going for walks on Sunday afternoons. Peter, home on a long weekend, was introduced to him and pronounced him unenthusiastically as a decent sort of chap. "But he's a bit of an egghead, isn't he, Mum?"

"Don't you like eggheads? Mark's awfully kind."

Peter looked alarmed. "You're not going to marry him are you, Mum?"

Eileen eyed her son narrowly. She had given up her contented life in the country for him. "I might. Would you mind?"

Peter looked aghast. "Oh, gosh, Mum!" Then that disturbing adult self-possession came over him. "Well, I suppose after all, you don't have me much now I'm at school. But he won't interfere in my affairs, will he?"

"I promise, only if you deserve it."

She would have liked Peter to be more enthusiastic. At least he wasn't hostile. The thought of that made her go into Mark's arms. He was gentle and sweet and it was so wonderful to be looked after again. There was no question of him taking Rupert's place. She was simply making another place for him.

They talked vaguely of marriage in the spring. The arrangements were still only vague when the letter came. Unexpected, unexplanatory, like a bomb dropped by an unknown enemy.

> Dear Mrs. Fairley, I wonder if you could lunch with me at the Savoy Grill at 1.15 next Thursday. It would give me great pleasure.
> Yours sincerely, Gordon Heseltine

Sheer curiosity took her there. She spent an agonised five minutes in the ladies' room deciding that her dark gray suit and green feather hat were definitely not *haute couture.* Then she remembered how much she disliked Gordon Heseltine. It would do him good to be seen with a woman who had neither mink nor real pearls. Her head was high as she walked into the restaurant.

He was at the table waiting for her. She found she hadn't forgotten the least thing about him, even the slight bluntness of his nose which just saved his face from being impossibly overbearing. It gave the suggestion of a plebeian ancestry. Probably his parents had been quite simple people.

"Mrs. Fairley! How good of you to come." He was smiling and holding out his hand. He even looked as if he were admiring the little feather hat. How disgustingly clever he was.

"I came to see what you wanted. I'm intrigued."

"It could be the desire for an attractive woman's company."

"It could be, but it isn't."

"You have honest eyes," he said. He stared at her for an embarrassingly long time. She remembered he had looked at her like that when he had come to the house. Then he said briskly, "Let's order. Then we can relax. You'll have a dry martini?"

She hadn't had a meal like this since the early days of her marriage. She wondered all the time what was coming, but she enjoyed the smoked trout, the grouse, the enormous sun-ripened peaches. She answered questions about Peter and his school, the flat she had found, her job. She even asked several herself about the white house in the country and the horses.

"Horses?"

"You were going to keep them in those fields you bought."

"Oh! That! I never bought that land, you know."

"You never—you mean you bluffed me!"

"I'm afraid so." The penetrating eyes did have a gleam of humor, not her kind but humor all the same. "Don't look at me like that. You know I did you a good turn. You're happier with a job, your boy is happier at this school you've sent him to."

"You try to cover up your unscrupulous method of getting your own way by turning it into a good deed! You're a hypocrite."

"So I am. But not all the time. Not at this minute. Mrs. Fairley—Eileen, my dear—I want you to marry me."

Her anger and indignation turned to pure astonishment. "Good heavens, are you mad?"

He laughed softly. He had the temerity to be enjoying himself. "Perhaps. I've always regarded myself as sane."

"But *marry* you! You don't love me. You scarcely know me."

"Both things can be remedied. Shall I explain?"

"No. Please don't. I'm not interested." To her surprise she was remorseful about hurting him. "I'm already planning to be married."

He took that with only the merest flicker of his eyes. For a moment she thought he was going to brush the information aside as unimportant. Then he said with the courtesy that she never quite expected from him, "I shouldn't be surprised. You're a very attractive woman. I blame myself for waiting too long. I knew at once the house was only complete with you."

Her moment of feeling for him, fragile emotion that it

had been, died at once. "But, unlike the house, I am not for sale."

"I keep seeing you in that room, in front of the fire-place, graceful, completely at home, your hair—leaf-brown, isn't it?"

"So there's something missing from the picture you bought?"

"There is."

"Then you'd better put it out of sight with your other Monets or whatever you own, and which I'm sure you never look at."

His hand, without warning, closed over hers. "Unfair. I live with my pictures. Shall we go?"

She sprang up, rubbing her crushed knuckles.

He deserved the rebuff, she told herself with fierce joy. Imagine telling that wicked lie about buying the fields simply to drive her out of the house. He would go to any lengths. But there were no lengths to which he could go to make a woman marry him if she didn't want to. He had at last met the immovable, the impossible. She wondered that he hadn't married already. He must be in his mid or late thirties. She thought he would have had as his wife some sleek, silky creature who paid for good dressing; not someone like her, a little shabby, with a transparently honest face and leaf-brown hair. Well, that was his impression of her, Eileen thought, studying her face in the mirror, trying to see what there was in it to attract a man like that.

Rupert had liked her quick and happy laughter, Mark her kindness. Gordon Heseltine would want something more subtle—oh, damn the man, what did he want?

A week later, on an evening when he usually called,

Mark telephoned. Eileen knew at once that there was
something wrong. His voice was guarded, almost guilty.

"If you can't come round, don't worry," she said.

"But it's not just tonight, Eileen. It's—well, I've a
chance of a job abroad."

"Abroad! But, Mark, how exciting! Where?"

"India: in a hospital with a big new research depart-
ment."

"India! Oh, Mark. What about Peter?"

His voice went on, uneasily, as if he had rehearsed
what he was going to say. "It's an important job. A
terrific challenge. Only—the catch is—they don't want
a married man."

"Oh! I see." Actually she had taken in the information, in spite of it being such a shock, with remarkable
speed.

"I'm sure they'll let me send for you later, Eileen, when
I've settled. But it's an opportunity I've always dreamed
about!"

"Of course. You must take it. Certainly you must take
it." Her voice was quite calm. She was even able to think.
There seemed to be a pattern about these events in her
life. "Can you tell me who offered you the job?"

"Well, no, actually I can't. At least, not just at present——"

"Don't worry. Leave me to guess."

She didn't make an appointment. With a smile and a
brisk air of importance she reached the room where the
top secretary sat behind a highly polished desk. "Mr.
Heseltine is expecting me," she said. "But I do want to
surprise him. Please! Don't spoil it!" She smiled coyly

and tiptoed to the great man's office. Great? Well, this young woman thought so.

She had opened the door, entered and closed it before he looked up. It almost seemed as if he had expected her. She was able to say pleasantly, "This time I decided not to wait for you to get in first. I just wanted to tell you that I never want to see you or hear from you again. If you thought sending my fiancé to India was going to leave the field open to you, you couldn't be more mistaken. I think you are the most abominably selfish and destructive man I have ever met."

"My dear Eileen!" He was coming towards her, his hand held out. "You weren't supposed to know anything about that. Did the foolish young man talk after all? Then you ought to thank me for saving you from him. He's brilliant, but emotionally weak. He hasn't the qualities that make a successful marriage."

"Haven't you heard *anything* I said?"

"Just as much as you heard me the other day at lunch. I want to apologize for that. It was bald and sudden. I had a great deal more to say if you would have listened."

Those unwavering eyes of his seemed to be looking into her very soul. There was no diffidence here, no kindness, no flexibility. "When will you listen to me?"

"Never!" she exploded. "Can't you understand? And if you attempt to see me I'll sue you for molestation."

"I had never visualized you angry. You're usually so calm. But anger becomes you, too. Do you know that I've never seriously looked at a woman before?"

"Then look hard, Mr. Heseltine, because it's the last time."

Her life was in a turmoil. She tried in vain to settle down. She realized now that she hadn't felt any deep emotion for Mark but it would have come, given a chance. Now she was truly alone. She clung to the thought of Peter's next long weekend. It would pull her out of her temporary lack of courage.

But Peter shattered her, almost at once. "I say, Mum, what do you think happened last Sunday? Mr. Heseltine came and took me to lunch at the George and Dragon."

"Mr. Heseltine!"

"Yes. He didn't have his chauffeur. He drove himself. He let me take the wheel for a while. Gosh, that car!"

Peter's blissful expression died as his mother turned on him.

"Peter, you're absolutely not to go out with that man again."

"But, Mum! I like him. He's different from old Mark. Sorry, Mum. You know what I mean."

"You mean you like Mr. Heseltine because he drives a Rolls and stands you an expensive lunch. You're a snob."

Peter frowned. "No. It isn't that. You can talk to him, sort of. Anyway, I had fish and chips. He said have what I liked."

She rang him up. She was put through so quickly that she suspected instructions had been given that if ever Mrs. Fairley phoned she was not to be kept waiting. "Mr. Heseltine, this is just the last straw. Corrupting my son. Haven't you any morals?"

"Corrupting?"

"Giving him expensive tastes. Showing him a world he'll never be able to afford. The next thing you'll be having the child suffering from a ridiculous case of hero worship." She was almost crying. "Please, please, leave him alone."

"In the first place, Eileen my dear, you underestimate your son. He's remarkably level-headed. In the second place, why do you assume he'll never be able to afford that kind of world? Unlikelier people than him have succeeded."

"Meaning yourself, I suppose."

"Meaning exactly that. I left school, such as it was, at the age of twelve. Since then I've found I could get on alone."

"I'm not interested in your life story."

"I know that. But I'm going to tell you some of it. Did you ever wonder why I was so determined to buy that very attractive but rather small and out of the way house?"

"I certainly did."

"It was because it was the first decent house I was ever in. I went to a rather deplorable council school—but never mind that. It happened there was one master who took an interest in underprivileged boys. Every other weekend he would take a couple of us to stay in his country house. He must have had private means. It was my first time away from—where I lived. I won't try to tell you the effect the house and garden had on me. I expect I thought it was paradise. But what really affected me was old Brown's wife. The place revolved round her. The way she behaved to us uncouth youngsters was something like a miracle. I remember never taking my eyes off her. A room was empty unless she was in it. She wasn't particularly beautiful. Just warm-hearted and gay and kind. I only went there once. But the memory of it has been a sort of fixation with me."

Eileen found that her hand was clenched round the receiver. "So when you saw the place for sale you had to buy it to recreate a dream."

"That's it. But I was too late."

"You're never too late, Mr. Heseltine. You make reparations."

"I was too late this time. You were there. And now I can't go into any of those damned rooms without seeing you. The empty house is no good to me."

"You mean you're substituting me for Mrs. Brown!"

"I'm not substituting you for anyone." The cultivated softness of his voice had given way to violence. The precocious, shrewd, wary, unscrupulous, sentimental boy showed through. Suddenly, just for that moment, he was human.

"But it's true what I said at the Savoy, Gordon." (Good heavens, she was even speaking to him as a human being.) "You only want me to complete your cherished picture."

"No. I'm giving up. You might like to note those historic words. I've never said them before."

"You're going to leave me alone?"

"I'm giving you back the house. I beg you to accept it as a gift. If you won't, then my very uncertain faith in human nature will completely disappear."

"I—I don't think I can——"

"Oh, hold your tongue! Haven't you said enough? Haven't we both said too much? My solicitor will send you the deeds."

The telephone clicked. He had gone. He was Gordon

Heseltine, millionaire, sitting in his luxurious office commanding his empire. The ghost boy was gone for ever . . .

When it came to the point, she couldn't leave London quickly enough. She, too, had had a fixation about that house, and it seemed a miracle that she was going back to it. Peter was quite amenable when he found the move wouldn't involve him leaving his school. "Sure, Mum. You like the country best, don't you? But you ought to keep a dog if you're going to be there alone."

Eileen rubbed his head affectionately. "I won't mind being alone."

All Mr. Heseltine's belongings had been taken away when she arrived. She walked the empty rooms, her footsteps echoing.

It would be all right when she had her furniture back in. Then she could settle down, not feel so alone. A dog might be a good idea. When Peter came home for his holidays they could go and choose one. In the meantime . . .

In the meantime the quiet rooms were strangely unbearable. Mrs. Higgins came from the village all day, but when she had gone the house seemed to die. Especially the drawing room. She could scarcely bring herself to go in there. She kept thinking that suddenly, in his unannounced way, Gordon Heseltine would appear and stand there filling the room with his personality.

Irrationally she kept remembering the pain of her crushed hand when he had squeezed it. He made one so acutely aware of him, so achingly, painfully alive. There would never be a moment's peace in his presence. Peace . . . who wanted peace?

Driven beyond reason, Eileen wrote and posted the letter. Her mind shut out what she had put in it. Something about, *It isn't a woman but a man who stands in this room and won't go.* And then, *Was giving me the house one of your more subtle methods? I don't know. When can you come . . . ?*

Obviously she had had a moment of mental aberration. She spent most of that night and all the next day walking about, going to the window to look up the country lane, so overgrown with foxgloves and Queen Anne's lace that there would scarcely be room for a Rolls to pass.

But when the big car did pull up at the gate, just as dusk was falling, she was suddenly quite calm. She saw the future shaping itself into its inevitable and only acceptable pattern.

# Fly by Night

In the early evening the girl arrived, crossing the church-yard to where the boat was moored at the river's edge. She carried a string bag crammed with packages that could mean only one thing—food.

The watching man, crouched behind the tilted tombstone, felt his mouth water. Earlier, he had taken a furtive look at the boat, ancient and unseaworthy, tipped sideways in the river mud now that the tide was out. It had seemed to be locked up and deserted. He had contemplated breaking into it to spend the night, but he had not expected to find food. He had imagined tightening his belt again and waiting until morning when the hue and cry would have died down.

But now the thought of food made him ravenous and prepared to take any risk. Particularly when the two thin and ingratiating cats suddenly appeared from nowhere to rub themselves round the girl's ankles, and follow her, with thin gull-like cries, down the plank into the boat.

She took a key out of her bag and unlocked the slanting door, then disappeared inside, leaving the door standing open.

It was too easy.

After compelling himself to wait ten minutes in case the girl should have had a companion who had lingered to pick up more supplies, the man warily emerged from his hiding place.

There was only one boat moored in this part of the river, beneath the stone wall that shut off the churchyard and the old grey church from the sight of the passing barges and the pleasure boats and the stretch of pungent black mud. Now, in the fading light, there were not even any barges passing, and the place was deserted. If the girl screamed there was no one to hear. But he hoped she would not scream. He did not want to have to use violence.

Thin and agile, with a tread as silent as the cats', he moved towards the shabby boat tilted crookedly in the mud.

Christine was astonished to think that she had not been here for a month. It was because of Mark, of course, and the fact that in less than a week it would be her wedding day.

Now that the day was so close she was full of uncertainties. She was almost sure that she did not want to be married. At least, not yet. Indeed, she could not think what had come over her since meeting Mark. She had always been jealous of her independence, but for the last three months she had forgotten that and everything else in her infatuation.

Then the previous night, for one uncanny moment, as if something in her had called "Halt!" she had suddenly seen Mark as a complete stranger. Who was he, this squarely built, very definite person who had swept aside all her qualms and simply asserted his possession of her? He did not like her to wear a certain fashion, so she stopped doing so. He was not happy about her going to what he called that "squalid hulk" on the Thames to paint, so naturally she did not go. He wanted her to read such and such a book, meet this friend or that, and certainly to stop looking paint-splashed and forgetful of her appearance as she had been when first they had met.

All this, indeed, he had accomplished. Until today. And suddenly resentment and rebellion and more than a little panic had risen in her.

This submerging of her personality and her freedom would last for the rest of her life if she married Mark. She couldn't do anything so tremendous without the most serious thought, and the only way to think was to get away from Mark. The place to do that was obviously the boat, the ancient *River Witch* that had long since abandoned her witchlike ways, and lay immobile at the water's edge, providing nothing but a dry cabin and a view.

But apart from Mark, Christine felt she should have come there more often because of the cats. Goodness knew what they lived on when she was not there. Nothing, by the look of their lean bodies and the way they had been lying in wait for her, rushing to greet her with tails erect and demanding voices. Luckily she had remembered them and brought some fish.

She was attending to them, setting down their plate of fish and filling a saucer with milk, when the voice came. "Don't make a noise! And put your hands up."

The first thought that flashed through her mind was that he was like one of the cats. Thin, hungry-looking, shabby, ready to snarl if annoyed. The difference was that he had, not claws, but a gun. The shape of it protruded from his pocket. And his hard, brilliant eyes had the wary, alert look of desperation.

Christine swallowed and managed to say steadily, "What do you think you're doing?"

"Nothing, if you do as I tell you. Get back in the cabin."

As she backed automatically out of the tiny galley, he closed the door and turned the key in it.

"Is there anyone else here?"

He must have known there was not before he came in. He had obviously been watching. So there was no point in lying.

"No one but the cats." (Lucky creatures, scoffing their food, thinking that all humans were the same, representing a free meal ticket. Nothing more or less.)

"Anyone likely to come?"

She grasped at that straw. "Yes. My fiancé. He's picking me up here."

"When?"

She saw his quick glance out of the window that gave a view of the track across the churchyard. She was acutely aware of the ominous bulge in the pocket of his shabby jacket, and all at once she knew that if Mark had been coming she would somehow have had to warn him.

"Not—for a little while," she gasped.

"What time? You must know."

Swiftly she thought. There was nothing here the man could want except what the cats wanted. Food. If she were to feed him, surely he would go. "In about an hour," she said.

The intruder relaxed perceptibly. It was obvious in the loosening of his meager body, the tired slumping of his shoulders. He was a little more than a boy, she thought, although he had a faint stubble of beard and his face was prematurely haggard.

"Good. Then you have time to get me a meal."

She lifted her chin. "At the point of a gun?"

"Listen, lady," he said wearily, "I just want food and if I get it quicker that way, that's fine."

He seemed to sway a little. He was about twenty, and he hadn't had any sleep for quite a long time. Or food. She was observant, and this was clear to her. He was too young to be so desperate, she thought inconsequentially.

"I've only got a loaf of French bread and some steak and salad," she said. "And coffee."

A faint distortion came to his lean face. It was the beginning of a smile, she realized.

"Lady, that makes it the Ritz. But get cracking. And I have the key to the door. So don't try any funny business."

She took a step towards the gallery, then paused to give him a long cool look. "You'd better sit down before you fall down. I promise not to climb out of the window, or even to burn the steak."

He scowled ferociously, lurching towards her. But she had been right in her assumption. His legs crumpled and he grabbed at the bunk for support. "Don't try any smart talk," he growled. "Just get that food."

The cats had finished their meal and were now giving her their thanks, weaving about her legs, purring loudly. Let's hope, she thought ironically, her other guest would not want to behave gratefully also.

But he would not. He would eat the food and then disappear into the night, a thin and desperate shadow. Seeking what? Heading where?

If it had not been for his gun she didn't think she would have been afraid. Not now, anyway, when she had seen his youth and sensed the curiously vulnerable quality of his roughness. "What have you done?" she called.

"Done? Whaddya mean?"

"You must have done something to be hiding like this. Had you been in the churchyard long?"

"Only since midday. I spent the night—never you mind where I've been. Just hurry with that food. And when I go you've not seen anybody. Understand?"

He had come to stand close beside her. His face suddenly wore a dreadful crafty look that brought all her initial fear surging back. The inexperienced young tough, she had read somewhere, could, from panic, act with the greatest violence.

"I understand," she whispered. "Though I don't know——" She stopped, refraining from putting any doubts in his head in case he might decide that the desperate course of silencing her altogether was the wisest.

"Look, here's some bread and butter. Go and begin while the steak's cooking. Do you like your coffee black or white?"

He gave his crooked, humorless smile. "Black, if it's all the same to you."

"Good. All the more milk for the cats. I wish you'd tell me why you're hiding like this. What have you stolen?"

"How do you know I've stolen something?"

But there was a furtive pride behind his sneering voice. So it had been a clever robbery, Christine thought, something he's feeling cocky about. Vaguely she supposed that burglars took a pride in a job well done just as much as a more honest person would.

"It's nothing to do with you, lady. The less said the better. Give me that grub. When did you say your boy friend would be here? Eight o'clock? You're not lying about that? It'll be the worse for him if you are."

Anger filled Christine—anger that Mark would not be coming because she had had to keep her own plans a secret. Why should she have to conceal the fact that she wanted to do such simple, innocent things as spending a night alone on her boat, and waking early in the morning to paint the dove-like colors of river and sky? As a result of this lack of understanding between them she was exposed to the unnecessary and foolish danger of a young gangster with a gun.

She lifted the sizzling steak out of the pan, and put it on a plate. He snatched it from her, not, she was sure, because he had never been taught good manners, but because his code would be to forget them. She turned back to the stove to attend to the coffee, and when that was ready, filling the air with its fragrance, the steak and the large hunk of bread had disappeared, and her guest was slumping across the table, watching her with a subtly lessened belligerence.

Perhaps he was not even twenty. She wasn't sure. Perhaps somewhere he had a mother who fretted about his strange comings and goings, but did not dare to speak.

"What's your name?" she asked.

"That's none of your business."

"Well, I'm frankly not consumed with curiosity. But I suppose your mother gave you a name once. It's no good keeping on looking out of that window. It's getting too dark to see anyone coming, anyway. I suggest you drink this coffee and get out of here quickly."

"Lady, you put the words in my mouth," he murmured, in his assumed jargon. "But don't think you're getting rid of me that easily. I'll be hanging about out there." He waved vaguely towards the churchyard. "I'll see if you try to leave here to warn anybody. So don't take risks."

She hadn't got to the stage of making plans like that, she realized. Her one idea had been to get rid of him, to send him on his furtive way. But now she wondered again what he had done, and if it were her duty to get in touch with the police. She had never been fond of the sport of pursuing hunted animals. But this particular species of animal was a menace to society. Or was he, she wondered, watching him drink the coffee, holding the cup in both hands and burying his face deep, like a child.

"More?"

He nodded. "And quick. Then I'm off."

The flame under the coffee pot had gone out. She had

to relight it, and wait a moment for the liquid to grow hot again. She realized suddenly that she was doing automatically what she would have done for a welcome and invited guest. Well—she had done as much for the cats, bringing them fish and filling them to repletion.

When she went back in the cabin she saw, with dismay, that she was not to get rid of her uninvited guest so easily. His head had fallen on the table and he was asleep.

For a moment she stood looking at him uncertainly. She'd shake him awake in a moment, she decided, and send him on his way. But no. Now was her opportunity to get possession of his gun.

Was he soundly enough asleep? He seemed simply to have passed out. She touched his arm tentatively, and saw that it would need a firm shake to bring him back to consciousness. It was safe enough to slip her hand into his pocket, the one that had bulged so ominously.

When she withdrew it she stood quite still, staring at what was in her hand. No gun. Not even a knife. Just a short stick with which he could do his desperate bluffing.

He was unarmed. And asleep. In spite of the unpleasant stubble of beard, his face was very young and defenseless. The frightened animal behind it was shut in out of sight. He did not even look peaky and starved and mean now, just innocent. His lashes were quite long on his cheeks. But he could do with a haircut and a shampoo. And a clean collar, and a better quality suit and new shoes. His shoes were the worst, and they probably would have to carry him a long way still, dodging down back streets and into shady pubs.

Christine stood thoughtfully with the make-believe gun

in her hand. One of the cats mewed to go out, and she
tiptoed to the door to unlock it and let the thin form
slip into the night. This was her chance to slip out, too.
She could lock the door behind her and come back
presently with a policeman to take care of her other
successfully trapped animal.

But instead of doing this she came back inside, relocked
the door, and then pulled the curtains across the windows
before lighting the oil lamp. Even this did not wake her
guest. He breathed quietly, not stirring.

Irrelevantly Christine thought of the kind of shoes Mark
wore. Hand-sewn, luxuriously soft leather, polished to
perfection, fashioned for the maximum comfort, even
though it was unlikely they would ever be subjected to
extremely hard wear.

If Mark were reduced to wearing synthetic shoes and
a synthetic suit, and the same shirt for a week or more,
how would he begin to behave?

That was not the point of this situation, of course. The
point simply was that the ancient laws of hospitality must
be honored. A guest should be allowed to eat and sleep.
So there was nothing to do now except wait until this
particular guest awoke.

This happened about three hours later, by which time
Christine was more than half asleep herself. She blinked
as the young man moved tentatively, then, coming fully
awake, leapt to his feet.

"Hey!" he whispered, as if there were other sleepers
close at hand, "what did you let me do that for?"

"I don't think anybody could have prevented it. You
were half dead, weren't you?"

"What's the time?"

"About eleven o'clock. And it's begun to rain."

"Eleven o'clock! Where's the boyfriend you were expecting?" He leaned over her, his face thin and menacing. "Have you played a trick on me? Has he gone for a copper?"

Christine smiled faintly. She was not in the least afraid now. "Look, Jimmy, or whatever your name is, calm down. I wasn't expecting anyone any more than you were carrying a gun. We were both bluffing. See? So you'd better get a bit more sleep before you leave."

His mouth fell open. For the first time the mask was off. He showed his young bewilderment. "You mean— stay?"

"Only because it's dark and wet out, and those shoes of yours don't look awfully waterproof. The tide's in. Feel it?"

The boat was rocking very faintly and there came a periodic slap of water against the bows. The smell of the dank black mud had gone, and now there was a fresh sea-smell that was invigorating and vaguely exciting.

The boy sat down slowly, not taking his eyes off her. "I don't get you."

"There's nothing to get, is there?" Her voice was crisp and matter of fact. "It's late and it's wet, and quite frankly I wouldn't turn a cat out. Where's your overcoat, Jimmy?"

"My name's not Jimmy." He licked his lips and said uneasily, "It's Robert. At least, that's what my mother called me."

Christine had a feeling that he had not used that simple, respectable name for a long time, and that he now produced it as the only honest thing he had to offer.

"And I pawned the last overcoat I had," he said belligerently.

"Oh, too bad. And you were cheated on the price, I'll bet."

"What do you know about pawning things?"

"You'd be surprised. Where do you live, Robert?"

"Now, look here, what is this? First, you act as if you hate me, and then you go all soft and talk like a Sunday-school teacher. What's it to you where I live?"

"Nothing at all. Sorry. I was only making conversation. Let's get some sleep."

His eyes had narrowed slyly, watching her as she lay curled up, fully dressed, on the bunk. "How'd you know I won't——" he paused, obviously searching for the polite word, not the graphic one that came most easily to his tongue.

"Because I trust you, that's why. Anyway, you're not that sort. You're decent."

"Me! Decent! But don't you know——"

"Oh, I know you're on the run at present. That's how you say it, isn't it? I suppose there was something you wanted, money or jewelry or something. Or else it's just a way you have of expressing yourself, as I do by painting pictures. We're all just humans, Robert. Some have better chances than others. I suppose, with an equal chance, you'd have been selling shares instead of stolen jewelry. The only thing about your way is that it'll get you nowhere. You do see that, don't you?"

"I've always wanted pretty things," he said rapidly. "When I was just little Ma used to say you can't have this and you can't have that. Because there was no money. My father drank. I haven't taken to the drink, but now when I see a pretty thing I take it. I started by picking the best flowers in the parks and people's gardens."

"Regular little horror, weren't you? But it didn't get you anywhere. Did it? Or you wouldn't be having to scrounge for food or go out in the rain without a coat."

She had left the lamp burning. She intended to leave it on all night. But she had been speaking the truth when she had said that she trusted him. She did, and it seemed important that he should know it. Also, she couldn't turn him out into the rain in that thin shoddy suit. He could go at first light.

"You haven't told me your name."

"It's Christine. I'm twenty-three and I'm being married next week. At least——"

"At least what? Don't you love this guy?"

He had a simple but direct mind. But beyond his ability to go straight to the vital fact, she sensed a hunger in his voice. He was envying Mark, whom he had never seen, or her, or everyone who had ever had dealings with that magical word. It was as far from him, he imagined, as the forbidden things in the shop windows when he had been a child.

Christine had thought she was going to admit to this strange, fly-by-night companion that she wasn't sure if she loved Mark. Instead, to her surprise, she heard her voice saying strongly, "I love him very much." It was as if she had just realized it.

"Will he be good to you?"

She nodded, her eyes stinging with sudden tears.

"Then that's fine, isn't it? What are you worrying about?"

"Nothing. Nothing at all. And neither will you when you fall in love."

"Me! Cor! That's a laugh."

"It's not a laugh at all. You will one day. Love's a pretty thing, too, Robert. And the advantage is that you don't have to steal it." She gave a laugh. "Now I *am* talking soft."

"Aren't you!" he muttered, but his voice had lost its derision and its certainty.

She hadn't meant to fall asleep, but unawares she did. The last thing she remembered about him was his watchful face staring at her, not in desperation, but in reflection. As if another element had come into his life, and he had to examine it suspiciously and with the greatest caution.

When she awoke it was morning, and he was gone. She knew that because the door hadn't been pulled quite shut.

She sprang up and hurried to look out. There was no one astir. The churchyard was empty. Even the two cats had disappeared.

It was not until she went back into the cabin that she saw the small square thing glittering on the table. She snatched it up. It was a silver box, a vinaigrette with a delicately scrolled edge, and still smelling faintly of some old perfume. Inscribed on the inner side of the lid were three words. She held them up to the light to read them. *Für meine liebling . . . .*

For my love . . . . Had he known what the words meant? Probably not, but he would have guessed. He would have known that someone long ago had given this little trinket to the woman he loved. But now both lover and loved were as anonymous as this young man himself, and only the gesture was left.

A few minutes later Mark arrived. She saw him coming across the churchyard and ran out eagerly to greet him. "Mark! Darling! How did you know I was here?"

"Simple deduction."

"Did you know last night, too?"

"What do you think?"

She searched his face. "But you didn't come?"

"If you'd wanted me you'd have asked me, wouldn't you? Just because we're being married, it doesn't mean you can't come here, or wherever you like, when you're in the mood to do so. Oh, I wanted to come. Don't think I didn't."

She flung her arms round him. "I'm so glad to see you."

He looked at her, puzzled. "You're different this morning."

"How am I different?" Her voice was wary.

"I don't know. As if something had happened to you."

"What could happen, down here in my old boat?"

"Actually, I don't want to alarm you, but something could. Apparently the police were hunting a thief not far from here last night. If I'd known I would have been down."

"Goodness! What had he robbed? A bank?"

"No. He was just a petty thief snatching some things from an antique dealer's. Nothing of much value. The police think he went to ground somewhere in Battersea."

"He could bury the things in the churchyard and come back for them long after," Christine murmured.

"Now you're getting fanciful, darling. You obviously need breakfast. Are we having it here, or shall we go back to my place? Do you know, you *are* different this morning."

Because she had looked into the dark? she wondered. Because in trying to project a little light into it for another person she had succeeded in doing so for herself?

"Perhaps I've learned to be more trusting," she murmured. "Let's have breakfast at your place. I'll just lock up."

But as if following a prearranged signal, the two cats appeared, springing over the wall, arching their backs and purring with pleasure. "Oh, wait a minute, Mark. I'll just have to stop and give the cats the rest of the fish I brought for them."

He watched her, his eyes tolerant. "What will they do if you don't come back here?"

"Oh, cats!" She thought of the thin boy's body slipping away into the early dawn, silent and secret—but having learnt enough trust to leave her the stolen silver box. Perhaps trusting a little more in the future, and then a little more, until at last he learned, like the cats, that his fellow creatures were not enemies. "They know how to take care of themselves," she said. "They'll survive."

# Summer's Love Affair

That double-edged remark was impertinent but appropriate. Mr. Jonas Todd may not have had immediate plans
for marriage, but he had never thought it necessary to
deprive himself of women, and was seen at fashionable
restaurants, night clubs and other playgrounds of the rich
with a succession of beautiful girls.

They might all be decorative, Serena had to admit, but
none of them, she thought passionately, was suitable to be
mistress (in the true sense of the word) of Stonehall.

That was for her.

She sat quietly, waiting to be summoned to her interview. She had seen plenty of photographs of Mr. Todd.
Again, the newspaper words described him accurately.

Chunky, dynamic, ruthless, though—when he chose—with a certain blustering charm. A Rochester looking for his Jane Eyre, one inspired journalist had commented when he had made his romantic purchase of Stonehall. `

And there she sat, her hands folded in her lap, a small inconsiderable creature with only one immediately outstanding feature, a jaw which was as determined as Mr. Todd's own.

A buzzer sounded. The secretary spoke into the intercom. "Yes, Mr. Todd. Very well, Mr. Todd." She looked across at Serena. "Mr. Todd will see you now, Miss Pennington."

The dynamic Mr. Todd advanced across an acre of carpet—no ostentation in this room either, but a great deal of expensive space—to shake her hand. His appearance was all that his photographs suggested, only more so, the gray eyes more acute, the jaw harder, the big square head more powerful, the heavy body too smoothly enclosed in the impeccable dark gray suit, expensive linen and handmade shoes. He was the complete concept of the self-made successful man. There was only one thing amiss. His carefully discreet silk tie had not been perfectly knotted, and had slipped slightly crooked. Almost as if, when he was alone, he had run a finger round the constricting collar.

Serena recovered from her nervousness. The man was human after all. When he asked, "What can I do for you, Miss Pennington?" she was able to answer composedly.

"It was good of you to see me, especially since I've come to ask a favor of you."

"Go ahead."

"You don't seem surprised."

"Well, I'm not dim-witted. I expect you've been reading the gossip columns. You've come to protest about someone like me buying Stonehall. I don't know what relation you are to the late owner——"

"Niece."

"I see. By the way, have you been to Stonehall lately?"

"No."

"Then you don't know the state it's in. In another couple of years, or less, it would be a complete ruin. I intend to put all that right."

"Doves in the dovecotes, water in the moat."

"Central heating to stop the decay," he said sharply. "Don't mock me, Miss Pennington. I know perfectly well what you're thinking. I wasn't born to a place like that. But what Stonehall needs now is money, not breeding."

The rough dynamic voice confused her. She wasn't sure whether it deepened or lessened her resentment. *Mr. Todd, the chip on your shoulder is showing . . .*

"But you're jumping to the wrong conclusions, Mr. Todd," she said. "I'm not objecting to your ownership. I'm delighted that someone with money has bought Stonehall. The last time I saw it, it broke my heart. But my uncle didn't care about it. He was always away. Anyway, he couldn't afford the repairs. But that's beside the point."

"What *is* the point, Miss Pennington?"

*I intend to marry you, Mr. Todd. That's the point . . .*

"No one knows Stonehall better than I do," she said smoothly. "When I was a child I spent all my holidays there and loved every stone of it. Apart from that, I know its history completely. Little personal things like the green curtains in the downstairs drawing room being changed to gold on the occasion of the visit of the Prince of Wales

in 1891. And how the Chinese silk happened to be hung
in the master bedroom. One of the Penningtons was a
great traveler. He brought home the Beauvais tapestries
in the hall, too, and the famous collection of Venetian
glass. The main drawing room was supposed to have
looked its best when it was painted white and gold. That
was done late in the eighteenth century under French
influence, but later the fashion was for dark brocaded
silk, and that's there still, though it's very shabby. I'd
like to see the walls stripped and painted white and
gold again, and the Fragonards and Watteaus returned.
I'd like all the four-poster beds put back in the bedrooms."

"Miss Pennington—" Mr. Todd's voice was mild—"it's
I, not you, who owns Stonehall."

"That's why I'm here. I want you to let me make the
house exactly what it used to be."

"The Beauvais tapestries, for one thing, are gone."

"I expected that. I heard Uncle Langley sold a lot of
things."

"And although I don't object to the white and gold
drawing room, I do to the Fragonards and Watteaus.
Whatever impression the newspapers may give, I'm not
a millionaire."

"Lesser known painters of that school would do."

He smiled faintly. "Thank you for that concession."

"But I couldn't compromise on the furniture. That must
be genuine, even if we have to comb England for it."

"You're going a little too fast. I haven't hired you yet.
Let's hear a little more about you. What's your present
job?"

She saw him looking at her neat but unexciting clothes

and knew what he was thinking. The poor side of the family, and even the late owner of Stonehall hadn't been the rich side. There was no longer a rich side, as he very well knew.

"I work at the British Museum."

"Antiquities seem to be your hobby. How old are you?"

"Twenty-five."

"Ambitions? Marriage?"

The question was irrelevant and a little impertinent, but she answered equably. "Certainly."

"You seem to know your own mind."

"It's a good idea."

He nodded thoughtfully. "I know mine, too. And I haven't bought Stonehall to found a dynasty, if that's what you're thinking. I've bought it because I like it. It's an old gem that needs resetting and I fancied doing that. When were you last there?"

"About ten years ago. Just before my uncle shut it up."

"Then we'll drive down at the weekend."

"We!" She couldn't hide her pleasure. "You are going to let me do this?"

"Hold your horses, Miss Pennington. I haven't decided yet. But if you can convince me that you know as much as you say you do, and if you don't bankrupt me with extravagant ideas like Fragonards or Watteaus, I'll consider your proposition." He was speaking into the intercom. "Miss Bell, will you show Miss Pennington out, and then bring me the file on the merger." He came round the desk, holding out his hand. "Goodbye, Miss Pennington. Give my secretary instructions as to where you can be picked up on Saturday morning. Ten sharp. My chauffeur will call for you."

He had asked if her ambitions were marriage. They always had been, but she had never imagined it would be to someone like him. Ruthless, crude, domineering, like a bulldozer. But why should she set herself up? She hadn't inherited the Pennington looks. She was like her Great-aunt Serenity whose sister had stolen the man she loved. Small, inconspicuous, hiding griefs . . .

Serena resolutely stopped her dreaming and sat down at her writing desk. She had letters to write to her three sisters, all married and settled down. She was the only one who had developed an undying passion for Stonehall.

*I am giving up my job and going down to Stonehall,* she wrote, *to help the new owner restore it. It's my intention to get it back for the family. I am not saying now how I am going to do this . . .*

When she had finished the letters she packed a bag with a selection of practical working clothes, and one party dress, black, very understated. Then she went to bed and slept soundly.

At five minutes to ten the next morning she locked her flat and carried her bag downstairs. Great-aunt Serenity had never traveled without her lapdog and her jewelry case which she never allowed out of her possession. Serena had a necklace of small real pearls to wear with the little black dress. That was the extent of her personal wealth.

Mr. Todd's chauffeur, who arrived punctually at ten o'clock, told her to nip in quickly because they had a long way to go, and the boss would expect to be there by midday.

Serena nipped in as ordered, and almost fell into the lap of a silvery-blonde young woman, expensively dressed.

"Oh, I'm sorry. I didn't expect——"

"Me? Why not? Jonas hates traveling alone."

"I'm going," Serena said stiffly.

"Then I suppose I'm a chaperon or something," the girl said absurdly. She was quite beautiful, and her accent was impeccable. One might have known that Jonas Todd, who had had the perspicacity to buy Stonehall, would also choose his girlfriends with discrimination.

"I'm Ann Greenslade. You're Miss what Pennington?"

"Serena."

"Elegant. I can see you're thinking my clothes are absurd for the country. But Jonas said we'd be eating somewhere civilized on the way home this evening. And I detest flat shoes and things." Her blue eyes flicked over Serena's shabby tweeds.

"I'm not expecting to be photographed," Serena said, and knew her sharpness was unjustified.

"How very astute of you," Ann said, "I expect you've seen me in the fashion magazines. It's getting that I can't go anywhere. Jonas likes it—I mean, when I'm recognized. He's the kind of man who doesn't feel complete without a good-looking girl on his arm. I find that rather touching. Don't you?"

They picked up Jonas at his Belgravia flat, and began the long journey. Jonas said he would sit in the front as he had some urgent papers to go through. If the girls wanted to gossip, would they put the partition up. Even so, separated by glass, Serena found his presence disconcerting. She didn't like his back view any more than she had done his front. Solid, egotistical, confident.

But the nearer they got to Stonehall the happier she became. She was already seeing in her mind the gray walls of the old house, the twisted chimneys, the tiled roof rosy in the midday sun, the dovecote, the herb garden, the roses Great-aunt Serenity had planted, the espaliered peach and apricot trees . . .

The glass partition slid down. "I hope you've got all your gen, Miss Pennington. We've only got a few hours. I want to be away by six."

"Serena looks awfully efficient," said Ann Greenslade.

The alert gaze flicked back again for a minute, resting on the small nondescript person with the impressive name.

But Serena could almost like him for the intent and possessive way he looked at Stonehall when they arrived. He was proud of it already, even if for all the wrong reasons. That was one emotion they would share.

He nodded gently when Serena said sharply to the fragile Miss Greenslade, "Don't stub out your cigarette on the floor. These floors are the original ones. I won't have them ruined."

Ann's blue eyes opened wide. "Goodness, Jonas. I thought this was your house."

"So it is. But do as Miss Pen—Serena says."

She didn't know whether he was trying heavily to be friendly, or whether her obvious concern for the house suddenly made him genuinely friendly.

"I say, Jonas, what a gorgeous room for a party," Ann said.

"Yes, isn't it. I intend to have one as soon as the house is ready. But wait till you see the ballroom and the terrace and the moat, which is going to be refilled."

"The water dances on the ceilings," Serena said, half

to herself. "I used to watch it when I was in bed with the measles. They put me in the Chinese bedroom. Do excuse me a minute. I must see if that perfectly lovely Chinese silk is still on the walls."

When she came back, Ann and Jonas were kissing halfway up the stairs. Serena's jaw hardened. With an effort she revived the feeling of happiness and peace she had had wandering through the empty, remembered rooms. She, this twentieth-century Pennington, was a composition of all her forebears who had loved Stonehall. Treasuring it and preserving it was her vocation. She would remember that when her husband kissed blonde girls on the stairways.

She shuffled her feet and made them look up. "Time's getting on, Mr. Todd. There are thirty-seven rooms to go over. I have my notebook. I'll make notes as we go."

"Ugh!" said Ann. "All those rafters and cobwebs. You can have them. I'll wander in the garden."

Serena said, "Then will you follow me, Mr. Todd? We'll begin on the first floor. One of the bedrooms has its original *toile-de-jouy*—it's still very beautiful. One of the Pennington ancestors was a French sympathizer at the time of the revolution. He gave refuge to several French emigrés until one stole his gold watch and his best hunter and never came back."

Jonas Todd said, "How old did you say you were?" The penetrating eyes, slightly quizzical, were staring at her.

"Twenty-five."

"You sound as if you're a hundred and fifty."

"It's just that I've read all the diaries and letters that survive. My Great-aunt Serenity was the best diarist. She never married, so her only interest was Stonehall. It was she who made the new rose garden." Serena pulled back the dusty curtains to look over the lawns and gardens, kneedeep in weeds. "It's still called the new rose garden although it's sixty years old. You'll need several men to get the garden into good shape, and then you'll need at least three permanent gardeners."

"By all means, if that drives away the old spinster's ghost."

"What have you against spinsters?"

"They have meddling fingers."

"Then you must be careful not to have any around."

Serena began to lead the way, but presently he was going ahead of her, opening doors, peering into cupboards, investigating unexpected stairways, testing window sashes, examining rafters. Reluctantly she had to respect his deep interest. When she began an anecdote about the widowed Pennington who had closeted herself in her bedroom, hung with melancholy shades of gray, for the rest of her life, he said curtly, "Cut the whimsey. There's a floorboard here that's going. Make a note. And what nitwit painted those rafters? They'll have to be stripped. There'll need to be at least six new bathrooms. This will be a long job."

"Give me six months," said Serena. "And a free hand."

"You'd have to engage architects, interior decorators, builders, eventually a staff."

"I know exactly what's required."

"I would expect to see plans and estimates."

"Of course."

"I want comfort as, well as antiquity."

"Naturally."

"How about all this Regency furniture and stuff?"

"I intend combing the country for it. I'll even get back some of the family portraits if you'll pay a reasonable price for them. I'll need a small car."

"I won't quibble about that. But I don't want any expensive item bought without consulting me."

"You can come down as often as you wish and see what progress has been made."

After a moment's pause, he said, "Well, this is my house now, remember."

"I promise I won't forget."

"I'm not sure I believe you. You've got a queer look in your eyes. However, if you know your stuff, as you say— if you don't I'll sack you. I never keep incompetent staff."

"My bag's in the trunk of your car. I'm staying here."

"In this empty house? There's no electricity, no hot water."

"I'll light a fire. There was always a supply of candles in the pantry. They'll still be there."

He laughed suddenly. "Aren't you afraid of ghosts?"

"My own family's?" She gave a small shrug.

"I believe you're like me," he said, surprise in his voice.

"In what way?" Serena asked coldly.

"When you get your teeth into a thing, you don't let go. What about your job?"

"I've given it up."

"You were that sure of me!" He looked angry for a moment, then decided to be amused and his great laugh echoed in the empty rooms. "I believe I've been soft-talked into something. But only because it suits me. And only for as long as it suits me. Now we'd better

go down. Ann will be yelling for us. It's getting dark and
she isn't as brave as you about mice and bats." His
hand came down heavily on her shoulder. "I like a pretty
woman to be a bit scared of things like that."

"But I'm not a pretty woman, am I, Mr. Todd?"

"No, you're not, but you're a Pennington whose ances-
tor sailed the Spanish Main. I believe I might be making
a mistake letting you loose in this house. But I guess
you're entitled to your love affair with it. So long as you
get it out of your system."

"I'll sleep in the Chinese bedroom," she said tranquilly.
"Ask your chauffeur to bring up my bag."

As first priority, she had the telephone connected. That
was not only because she needed it for ringing tradesmen,
but so that she could report to Jonas regularly. She intended to keep him aware of her existence. Stonehall
might be his hobby, his *folie de grandeur*, able to be
pushed out of his mind when business absorbed him. But
she was another matter. Her voice was going to become
familiar to him, certainly much more familiar than that of
the succession of pretty girls who would accompany him
on the long drive down whenever he chose to visit his
estate.

Serena anticipated the girls, but decided that she would
be a poor creature if, by the end of the summer, Jonas
did not occasionally come down alone. Especially as the
house began to emerge in all its remembered beauty.

She had extraordinary luck in finding the right materials
and the right workmen. The little white car Jonas had
sent down became known all over the county as she
searched for furniture, old paintings, antiques. Every week
she accounted to Jonas, telling him of her purchases. His

voice barked orders down the telephone, and on his visits they pored together over designs, figures, swatches of material.

The house was their contact, their love. He was growing as absorbed in it as she was. This was exactly what she had intended. She became so accustomed to his square figure, his undistinguished face, his brows beetling over the acute eyes, that his appearance no longer disturbed her. She didn't think he noticed hers any more than he ever had. But he would . . .

Exactly six months later, as she had promised, the work was finished. The refurbished rooms, the shining diamond-paned windows, the cropped lawns and clipped yews, the neat garden beds, the water gleaming darkly in the moat, the lazy twists of smoke from the chimneys, the doves fluttering with a clapping of snowy wings, the stable clock striking the hour—all might have been waiting for the return of Sir Francis Pennington from the Spanish wars. Instead, a stream of cars slid over the drawbridge, and a horde of gay, glittering, noisy people were let loose in the lovely rooms. Serena took down the little black dress that had hung all summer in the wardrobe of the Chinese bedroom, put it on, took care with her makeup, looked at her small unspectacular Pennington face in the mirror and knew that now was the moment. Or never.

Because if once she had cherished a sentimental love for Stonehall, this summer had increased it to a passion. She was prepared to pay any price, even to marry Bluebeard himself, to make the house her own. And Jonas Todd was not Bluebeard, he was only an uncultured country boy who had grown up with a flair for making money.

She saw Jonas standing in front of the fireplace in the hall, the portrait of the Elizabethan Pennington hanging behind him. He looked affable and pleased with himself. His broad shoulders and square heavy body actually looked rather well against the enormous Tudor fireplace. He had something of the same swashbuckling look as Sir Francis Pennington. And Sir Francis, Serena recalled, had been a farmer's boy, too, before he ran away to sea.

Her heart bumped suddenly when Jonas saw her. "Oh, there you are. Everyone's asking who the genius is who has done the house. I've assured them that everything's correct, down to the last teaspoon." He studied her. "Is that your party dress?"

The black dress seemed skimpy and somber among all the shimmering satins and brocades. "I'm only the housekeeper."

"And not that any longer. You've done a magnificent job, but it's finished. Come and have some champagne. We haven't discussed payment yet."

"Oh, I have a bill."

He looked at her again. "You say that as if you intend to bankrupt me. And I wasn't making derogatory remarks about your dress. It's fine. It looks right."

"Right for what?"

"Not the housekeeper. I've never seen you dressed up before. You're not pretty, but you've got something."

"The Pennington look," said Serena.

"You're arrogant, aren't you?"

"Oh, yes." She took the glass of champagne he handed her, sipped it, and said, "I found you Pennington portraits, but they aren't enough."

The amusement went out of his eyes. They became intrigued, a little wary. "I believe you think the house needs you as well!"

"Yes. It does."

"Would you want to stay here as my housekeeper? You're rather young. And unattached. People would talk."

"I wasn't suggesting staying as your housekeeper."

He suddenly gave his great guffaw. "Come outside. We can't talk in all this racket. Are you by any chance proposing to me?"

The terrace was crowded, too. There were at least two hundred and fifty people at the party, and no place would be free of them except perhaps Great-aunt Serenity's rose garden, where it was dark, and only accustomed feet could find the paths.

Serena led the way there. She turned and saw the dark silhouette of the house, its twisted chimneys against the pale sky, and a great surge of emotion shook her.

Her voice actually trembled as she said, "Yes, I am proposing to you. In all truth I am. I know you have feelings against marriage. You're suspicious about women's motives. And quite rightly. They do have them. Most of them would be interested in your money. I'm not. I only want Stonehall. And you would like to have it complete. It can only be that way with a Pennington mistress. Don't you agree?"

She expected him to give his crass bellow of laughter. Instead he was so silent that she became nervous again.

"That kind of marriage won't need to worry you. It will really be like owning another piece of property."

"Or an art treasure?" He spoke at last, his voice sarcastic. "Are you beautiful enough? What happens when you get old?"

"I'll try to age as well as Stonehall."

He said in astonishment, "I believe you've had this in your head from the beginning."

"Yes, I have. But I've done my share. I've given you the house and the garden, the family portraits, even the doves in the dovecotes as you wanted them. The stable clock strikes the hour again. I've brought the place to life. I want to keep it alive. I really wouldn't worry you at all."

She knew he was interested. She could feel his concentration. His quick brain was seeking out the advantage to himself in this odd situation. "Other women?" he asked. "Come, now. If this is a business arrangement, you can't object to that."

She knew she did, unexpectedly. Something stung. "I don't like scandal."

"I can be discreet."

"But most women can't. I couldn't have scenes."

"I never make a contract that has endless stipulations."

"This is the only one. No scandal."

He suddenly took her arm and fondled it, rubbing his fingers up and down it as if she were some *objet d'art.* "I don't think I fancy being married to a house."

"But you must admit Stonehall needs a mistress. A housekeeper left to idle while you're away? A butler who drinks your best port? How can you want to own it if you're not going to treat it properly?"

"I suppose you'll say next that you want four daughters, making history repeat itself."

She drew her arm away. He had stung her again. She

did want four little girls. "You're not in love with anyone else."

"Love! What's that? I never knew it. Neither did my parents. My father drank and beat my mother every Saturday night." His voice was coarse and should have revolted her.

Instead, she felt a twist of pity. "Well, then——" she began, less surely.

"Well, then, there's a party on and I'm the host. We'd better go inside. I'll think over your suggestion. I won't dismiss it out of hand. You've done a splendid job in every other way. You may even have the right idea. I may find I can stand being a husband on sufferance."

"I didn't mean that."

"Then what did you mean, I wonder?"

All the rest of the evening and into the small hours, he watched her. The party got wild and a little drunken. The rafters rang as they could not have done since the heyday of the Penningtons. Jonas danced a great deal with one girl, a spectacular redhead, but over her shoulder his eyes watched Serena with an interested, impersonal, weighing-up look. Beneath his gaze she was uncertain for the first time, chilled by her own cold-blooded planning. Had she let her obsession for Stonehall blind her to practical realities? Could she face the bedroom (even though it were her beloved Chinese one) and the breakfast table in Jonas Todd's company for the rest of her life?

The last car roared over the drawbridge. The guests had gone.

Jonas came looking for her, and found her on the terrace. "How long have you been here?"

"I don't know."

"Well, come inside before you freeze to death. You're not as immortal as this house you're so crazy about."

She came towards him slowly. She was stiff with cold. He took her arm and led her inside, shutting the long doors behind them. "Come in by the fire."

"It's time to go to bed."

"A last drink. I've told the servants to leave the clearing up."

"Aren't you going back to London?" she asked.

"Why? I suppose I can have a bed in my own house?"

"You've never stayed before."

"I waited until the place was comfortable. I must give you credit for making it that."

They were employer and employee. She said formally, "The party was a success."

"Terrific. No one fell in the moat. Although you look as if you had. You're all gooseflesh." He threw another log on the fire and poured brandy. "You look too small," he said.

"Too small?"

"For childbearing. I'd want to be sure of a son."

"But I'm not too small," she said passionately, her hands measuring her pelvis. "All the Pennington women have been small, but they've had large families. One had eleven, and her waist was eighteen inches."

His eyes narrowed into their assessing stare. "I've been watching you. You look the real thing, I must admit. You made the other women look showy. You're not pretty, but you've got an air. I once had a whippet, a delicate shivering little thing. You remind me of her.

My father made me get rid of her, though. Said she didn't earn her keep."

"I'd earn mine."

"Housekeeping? There'd be more to it than that. Look at me. Take a good close look at me." Embarrassingly, he thrust his face at her, turning it to different angles. "I'm no oil painting, am I? No breeding there. Look at my peasant's hands. I challenge you not to wince when I put them on you."

"I wouldn't!" Serena was so indignant that he gave his great laugh.

"You know, I never really saw you until this evening. I used to tell people I'd got a girl who seemed to be a bit of a nutcase doing my house in the country. What did you say about me?"

"Why—nothing, except that you got what you set out to get. You were a bulldozer. You made other men seem effeminate."

"You said that!"

His pleasure was suddenly so naïve, so transparent, that she murmured in embarrassment, "It's true. The house always seemed empty when you had gone. You made such a noise."

"I didn't think you'd be a girl who liked noise. Didn't you think it vulgar?"

"The first Pennington," she said, "was a farmer's boy who ran away to sea. Did you know that?"

"He must have been a pirate if he could afford to build this."

"The spoils of war. He fought with Drake and was knighted by Queen Elizabeth. A dynasty has to start somewhere."

"This farmer's boy prefers to start his own, if he must, not latch on to an old one. If you love this ancient dump so much, I'll give it to you."

She was deflated, the wind taken out of her sails. "Don't be absurd. How could you do that?"

"You've made your case. I'll return it to the Penningtons. It belongs to them. I'm an outsider who can be allowed to save it from demolition, to give it a vulgar transfusion of money. But that's all."

"I didn't mean anything of the kind!"

"Didn't you?"

"No, I did not!" She stared into his hard eyes, and cried exasperatedly, "How could I have expected you to understand? You're only——"

"One of the *nouveau riche*? You see, I know my French."

"Oh, Jonas Todd! That chip on your shoulder! I saw it when I first saw you."

"And I saw the ice cubes in your veins, blue ones, at that."

"How do you think I could possibly accept a property worth a quarter of a million pounds?"

"How could I accept your form of payment?" he retorted. "An iceberg in my bed. How do you get sons from an iceberg?"

"You didn't want sons until I raised the subject. You said you got along very well without marrying."

"So I do."

"Then get on with it," she said furiously. "Start now by sitting alone at your fireside. Because I'm going upstairs to pack my bag."

She wouldn't have thought anyone so heavily built

could move so fast. In a split second he was barring the door. "Hold it, you crazy little cat. I'm just beginning to enjoy this talk."

"Well, I'm not. I've humiliated myself enough."

"Will you stay if I apologize?"

"For what?"

"For saying you had ice in your veins. I can see now that your blood is a good healthy red. Look at your cheeks."

She didn't need to. She could feel them flaming. "That's because I have a bad temper. I should have told you."

"The Pennington temper, I haven't a doubt."

"You're laughing at me."

"Sure. Isn't that nice? It makes you human."

"I always was."

"No, you weren't. You were a piece of furniture in this house. And do you know something? You'll go back to being that if I don't keep you alive."

"What rubbish!"

"I'm not sure we should ever spend more than three months of the year here. May, June and July, perhaps."

"Jonas!" she whispered.

"Don't lick your lips. You think you've got round me. You're a devious female. I don't think I'll ever be sure of you. And I don't like that, although I admit it's intriguing. I might find I wanted to make you pay for it."

"How?" she asked.

"I don't know yet. Let's try a kiss."

She lifted her face quite calmly, then was amazed at her innocence in thinking she could remain cool and collected. She might have confused sensations (distaste, disgust, a surprising pleasure?) but none of them would be calm.

"Well," she said, her voice tripping.

"Try again," he said.

She did so, then pulled herself away. "Don't start thinking that one kiss——"

"Two kisses," he retorted.

"Two kisses, then, make one start getting sentimental."

"Oh, I'm not as naïve as that. But they do give an indication as to compatibility."

"Well, now you know that I don't wince," she mocked.

"You'd tolerate it?"

"I give you my word."

So suddenly that she gasped, he gripped her shoulders, then his mouth forced her lips apart. When he let her go she almost fell. "That's not for fun, that's for real," he said. "That's how it would be. If I have a wife, she won't be treated like something that might break."

"I won't break," she said steadily.

"I'll have no passiveness. It's either love or hate."

"I hadn't wanted an indifferent husband either," she said, surprising herself.

"But you had never thought of a man like me as your husband until this summer, had you? Had you?" he demanded.

She knew one thing already—that she would always have to tell him the truth. "No, I never had. But I've never minded being proved wrong."

His expression had changed. It was no longer hard, it was quizzical, almost tender. After a long time he said, "Don't think I've made up my mind. I haven't. But since you've spent the summer preparing the ground, now you can spend the winter convincing me that something will grow in it. Something good. Maybe it will, at that." He held out his hand. "Come. We'll drink a toast to the summer's love affair. Stonehall."

She followed him slowly to the fire. She was thinking that she couldn't wait for the winter to come.

# The Hopeful Traveller

When Aunt Adelaide's small holding of apparently worthless mining shares, left to her by her husband, suddenly skyrocketed in value, she decided there was only one way to spend such an unexpected windfall, and that was to take her long-planned trip back to England.

She did not, however, mean to travel alone, and, being a generous person, instantly decided on two things. She would invite her sister Ruth and her niece Claudia to accompany her. Ruth would be a congenial companion and between them they would contrive to give Claudia, who was inclined to be a little too serious, the time of her life.

Being a person of impulse, she lost no time in "summoning" Ruth and Claudia to her home.

Claudia, who was not so impulsive—somewhere, over the years, a good deal of caution had crept into her nature —listened in astonishment to the conversation of her two excited aunts.

"We'll sail on the *Corinthian*," Aunt Adelaide declared. "Deck cabins and lots of clothes. We must begin shopping. Claudia, you must ask for three months' leave. If they won't give it to you, you must quit your job!"

"Quit!" gasped Claudia.

"Why not? You can get another. I never was very happy about the one you have, anyway. Nothing but pictures and statistics. It tends to mummify a young girl."

"But, Aunt Adelaide, I love my job. I love the pictures. I'm an authority on Rembrandts. . . ."

"That's what I'm saying," Aunt Adelaide went on smoothly. "What you need is a cultural tour abroad. And not only cultural. Make notes for me, Ruth. Make a heading: Claudia's wardrobe. Start with dance dresses."

"But, Aunt Adelaide, if I travel with you two—oh, I'd love it enormously; you know how I adore you both— but who do I dance with?"

"Ah-ha!" said Aunt Adelaide, beaming, "that's the crux of the matter. You'll be having a delightful sea trip. It's up to you who you dance with. I scarcely need to remind you that both Ruth and I met our husbands on board ship. Your Uncle George was assistant purser on the *Leander* and your Uncle Eric fourth engineer on the *Duchess of Carlyle*. Fateful trips, weren't they, Ruth, honey?"

Aunt Ruth nodded in happy retrospect. "That's the word, Addie, Fate!"

Claudia leaned forward. "Aunt Adelaide, this is terribly sweet of you, but what makes you think the same thing will happen to me?"

"I agree, one can't be sure. But you'll have everything on your side, pretty clothes, romantic music, moonlight over all those vast miles of ocean, time . . . if ever you're to fall in love, Claudia, it will be then."

"Why not right here in Boston?"

"Well, my darling child. . . ." Aunt Adelaide's expressive eyes spoke the story of Claudia's lack of a successful romance. Both quizzical and frank, they suggested that dear Claudia did not try very hard. She was allowing herself to grow bookish and absentminded, to neglect her appearance, to be overcritical of perfectly nice young men, and lazy about keeping herself in circulation. For instance, having to work late in an art gallery was no excuse for missing parties. Let the art gallery find plain, middle-aged women to do overtime. Claudia was only twenty-six.

"But twenty-six without a steady boyfriend," Aunt Adelaide added. The setting was the trouble. No dry-as-dust picture gallery would do. What Claudia needed to bring her out was the glamour of shipboard life. There, true to the family tradition, she would find herself.

Claudia sensed all this at once. She had a great deal of rather stiff-necked pride and she was resentful. So Aunt Adelaide didn't think she could get an offer of marriage without the aid of a luxury sea voyage? If that was the only way, then she had better remain unmarried. Men bored her, anyway. They were so sure, so eager to talk about themselves, so certain a pretty girl should hang on their words, so boringly athletic, so unappreciative of any painting that was not the current fashion. . . .

She had decided she would be happier devoting her life to the old Masters, Rembrandt particularly, than marrying one of these brash, insensitive young men.

"Aunt Adelaide, it's awfully sweet of you to ask me but, if this is to be just a matchmaking trip, I'll only disappoint you, so I'd better not come."

"Not only a matchmaking trip, dear. Oh, I do admit your Aunt Ruth and I have these silly dreams. We feel responsible for you since your parents died. But you must remember we were English before we married and neither of us has been home since. You're half English too. You ought to see London. You'll love it. Put young men on the list, Ruth, next to dance dresses. I admit I find them highly important. But add England, too."

"And the picture galleries," put in Aunt Ruth slyly. "Did you know, Claudia, there are nineteen Rembrandts in the National Gallery alone?"

"*Are* there really?" Claudia wavered.

"Oh, very well," said Aunt Adelaide tartly. "Add the Rembrandts after England. But I'm making a guess that, by the time Claudia gets to London, she'll be very happy to leave them last on the list."


A month later they set off. Aunt Adelaide and Aunt Ruth, neither of whom had a deep interest in clothes, traveled light, but Claudia had nearly as many bags as a film star. It was no use to protest. Aunt Adelaide had enumerated the variety of shipboard activities, and nothing was unprovided for. In a few days, Claudia reflected gloomily, she would daily have to change at least five times.

The clothes, the latest haircut, and the undeniable excitement about going to London, had made her ravishingly pretty.

"What did I say?" asked Aunt Adelaide triumphantly.

"There still has to be a suitable young man," murmured Aunt Ruth.

"If the dear child goes on looking like that there'll be plenty."

"But what will they be?" Aunt Ruth had more than a fair share of Claudia's own caution. "It might well be that the old saying will be true: 'It's better to travel hopefully than to arrive'."

The *Corinthian* was a floating hotel. Like a hotel, it housed all types.

The kind of frank-faced, clean-cut young men whom Aunt Adelaide and Aunt Ruth were looking for were, unfortunately, scarce. Those there were seemed to have attractive girls already hanging on their arms—and their words. Claudia was secretly amused and relieved. She wore the pretty clothes the aunts had spent so much trouble finding for her, and drifted about looking supercilious and bored. If she could have worn her own shabby clothes she would have looked just as bored. But the Fifth Avenue smoke-gray chiffon and azure satin dance dresses could not help adding both sophistication and superciliousness.

Several middle-aged and elderly men made strenuous passes at her. The only possible young one, whom Aunt Adelaide had finally snared to share their table, proved to be a complete failure. His handsome face covered what must surely be a vacuum.

The aunts were in despair. They fluttered round the

ship's officers but, when at last one could be secured for drinks, Claudia had, infuriatingly, disappeared. By the time she was dug out of her sun-trap on the top deck, nicely isolated from everybody, the officer had had to go back on duty.

The last day of the voyage came, and England lay on a cloudy horizon.

"I don't know," Aunt Adelaide lamented. "All I can say is, times must have changed. When we were young girls on our first voyage———"

"Perhaps you weren't girls like me," Claudia interrupted gently. "I don't want to be kissed on the boat deck late at night just because I'm at sea."

"Claudia, I declare, you're as pretty as a picture and you wear those new clothes like a dream. But you just don't seem normal not to want a romance on board ship."

Claudia looked at her with her rueful, honest gaze.

Aunt Adelaide sighed.

"Oh, very well, Ruth, put those Rembrandts at the top of the list. But I'm telling you, Claudia, we hope for better things on the return voyage. You just can't go on disappointing us."

London was shrouded in mist and drizzle. The aunts shivered and got themselves cozily installed in an expensive Mayfair hotel as quickly as possible.

"How can it be so chilly in midsummer?" complained Aunt Adelaide. "I'd forgotten the atrocious climate. I'm not sure I'm going to enjoy being back home."

"It'll improve," said Aunt Ruth. "After all, we don't need to go out in the rain."

Claudia's cheeks were pink with enthusiasm. She looked prettier than ever, thought Aunt Adelaide crossly. And for whom? Those dark old paintings in a picture gallery!

"I'm going out," she announced. "I just can't wait to see those Rembrandts."

"Then don't ruin your good clothes. Put on something old."

"I didn't bring anything old except my raincoat. Isn't it lucky I brought that?"

She bent to kiss her aunts on their petulant cheeks.

"Don't wait lunch for me. I may stay quite a long time."

How would she get to the National Gallery? By bus, of course. The hotel porter told her the number to catch, and, feeling as if she had set out on an exciting adventure, Claudia boarded it and climbed to the top deck.

The conductor came for her fare. She had a purseful of English money, but had neglected to examine the value of the different coins.

"To the National Gallery, please," she said.

"You're going the wrong way, miss."

"What?"

"You should have caught a bus on the other side of the road." They were rocketing along through the traffic. The conductor saw her bewilderment and added kindly, "Give me a three to Hyde Park Corner, then you can cross over and catch a nine."

"He means a threepenny ticket," said a voice beside her. "Here, this is three pence. I'll show you where to get off."

Claudia leaned back gratefully. She hadn't even noticed she had sat beside a young man.

"Thank you so much. I thought English was spoken in London but it sounds like a foreign language!"

"You'll get used to it." The young man looked very English indeed. He wore a bowler hat, but instead of an umbrella, he had a violin case.

Interesting, thought Claudia. And she rather approved of the thick dark hair that showed beneath his hat. It was refreshing after all those uncompromising crew-cuts.

"Would you like me to explain our money?"

"Oh, I would. I'm so stupid. I just got some dollars changed at the hotel desk and didn't examine what they gave me. I was so anxious to start out. I just can't wait to see the Rembrandts."

The young man gave her a rather odd look. He had long dark eyes that gleamed. He thought, of course, that she was just another tourist, mad about culture. Well, so she was, in a way.

"They've been there a long time," he said. "Ten minutes more won't do any harm."

"Why?"

"We've just passed Hyde Park Corner, where you should have changed. Come as far as the Albert Hall with me, and I'll explain our money system."

"Oh! Oh, very well. It's kind of you. Won't I need another fare?"

"I'll fix it. Now, look, this is three pence, as you've already discovered. This is six pence, worth twice as much as three pence."

"Do all English men wear those adorable hats?" Claudia asked, looking at his.

His brows rose a little, coldly it seemed. He thought she was laughing at him. But she wasn't.

No, he didn't think so after all, for the gleam had appeared in his long dark eyes.

"Some," he said finally.

"You've missed your stop, miss," came the conductor's voice severely.

"Two to the Albert Hall," said the young man with crisp unintelligibleness. "I say, are you really keen on Rembrandts?"

"Crazy about them."

"Oh!" He didn't sound disappointed as much as genuinely surprised. "Interesting. Then you should like ours. But let's go over this money again. Now you tell me what these coins are."

It was very confusing indeed and by the time she had got them correctly the young man was saying, "This is our stop. We'd better start getting down. Do you mind telling me where you're staying?"

"The Dorchester."

"Oh!" For a moment his eyes did hold disappointment. Or was it disbelief?

Her raincoat really was pretty shabby, and he couldn't know of all those fabulous clothes foolish, romantic Aunt Adelaide had bought.

He followed her down the stairs of the swaying bus, and eventually on to the street.

"You get your bus over there. See that stop? A number nine. Enjoy the Rembrandts. So long, Miss America!"

He had thought she was fooling him. All that wide-eyed innocence about money, and her shabby coat, and then turning out to be probably an oil king's daughter. She shouldn't have said she was staying at the Dorchester.

But she was, wasn't she, and if he had wanted to see
her again . . . oh, she hadn't told him her name!

The Rembrandts were marvelous, of course, but Claudia scarcely saw them. She was back at the hotel in time
for lunch.

"Honey, didn't you like them?" exclaimed Aunt Adelaide.

"Oh yes, they were wonderful."

"You didn't spend long there."

"No. I guess I was hungry."

"But, honey, you're not eating anything. Don't you
like roast beef?"

"It's very good. . . ."

"Then eat it, child!"

"She's caught cold, I expect," said Aunt Ruth gloomily.
"Everyone does in London. It's the changeable weather."

Claudia leaned forward desperately. "Aunt Adelaide,
I don't suppose anyone was enquiring for me—no, of
course, they couldn't be."

"Who were you expecting? You never told me you
knew anyone in London."

"I don't. At least, I didn't until this morning. I met
a young man on a bus. He was very kind. . . ."

Aunt Adelaide had drawn herself up instantly. Her face
was full of astonishment and disbelief.

"On a bus! Claudia! I thought you'd have more sense.
One doesn't pick up men on a bus!"

Claudia flushed, crying, "I don't see what's the difference, a ship or a bus. You'd willingly have me dance
and drink and even kiss strange men on a ship. But I only
had a perfectly ordinary conversation with this young

man. He explained English money to me. He was very kind. He didn't even tell me his"——her voice trembled—"his n-name."

"I should think not!"

"I told him I was staying at the Dorchester, so he thought I was M-Miss America."

Aunt Adelaide's lip quivered. Humor began to sparkle in her eyes.

"Ruth, I believe the child has something after all. Her very first day in London, too." She turned to Claudia. "But not on a bus, Claudia, honey. That's much too ephemeral. A ship now, and you could meet this young man again at lunch or dinner, or in the cocktail bar. There's some sort of future to it. Now cheer up, dear. All isn't lost. After all, if this young man could think you were Miss America in that quite dreadful raincoat, what will everyone think of you in a Dior dress."

"A Dior dress," said Claudia blankly.

"Nothing less. I intended it as a surprise. We'll go shopping this afternoon. You'll wear it the second night out on the return voyage. Now isn't that something? Ruth, didn't I say the Rembrandts weren't important? Put Dior at the top of the list."

But after lunch Claudia said she had a headache and could the shopping be postponed.

She really did have a headache, but also she had a funny frightened feeling that buying the Dior dress would be committing her to what Aunt Adelaide desired——the successful sea voyage home and the nice American beau tailored to fit Aunt Adelaide's requirements.

Her heart wasn't in it, Claudia thought miserably. She wished it were, but it wasn't.

She kept thinking of long bright dark eyes and a courteous English voice, and that absurd, formal bowler hat. But not the rest of the uniform, the rolled umbrella. A violin case instead.

A violin case!

Claudia sat upright on her bed. Why, of course! The young man was a musician. He was playing at the Albert Hall, probably in an orchestra. This morning he must have been going to a rehearsal.

She only had to go to a concert to see him again. It was as simple as that.

"Claudia dear, your Aunt Ruth and I are seriously worried about you." This was a week later. "We didn't mind the Rembrandts so much. After all, they are your job. But this passion for Bach and Beethoven, when there's all the world to be enjoyed! I don't know who you get this intenseness from. I'm sure it isn't from your mother. She was like Ruth and me, ready to have fun. Do be a good child and start having fun. That's why I brought you to London. Now surely you're not going to another concert!"

Claudia nodded bleakly.

"Yes please, Aunt Adelaide. I want to. I really do."

"Oh, dear, I believe that is your way of having fun," Aunt Adelaide sighed. "Then why not try the Festival Hall some night, just for a change? At least it would be different surroundings."

"I'm not interested in surroundings," Claudia said. She managed to smile. "Don't worry, Aunt Adelaide. I expect I'll get it out of my system eventually."

"I do hope so, I'm sure. But couldn't you just relax and fall in love?"

Relax! thought Claudia. But falling in love was the most unrelaxing thing she knew.

Twice at the Albert Hall she thought she had seen him in the front row of the violinists. But in evening dress and without his bowler hat she couldn't be sure. She could never sit near enough to the orchestra and she couldn't ask for him because she didn't know his name.

All this going to concerts was quite pointless, as Aunt Adelaide had said. And anyway if she were to find him, what could she say? He had almost certainly by now forgotten all about her. Travel madness had really seized her, not on board ship, but in a strange city.

She must really come back to earth. Tonight, she told herself firmly, was the last night she was going to a concert.

It poured with rain. She had had an early dinner with the aunts, and then put her raincoat haphazardly over her dinner dress. She was wearing the simple black chiffon, because Aunt Adelaide, having bought her all those delectable clothes, liked to see her wearing them. If it were too dressed-up for the Albert Hall, her raincoat successfully covered it.

As usual, the evening was abortive. No one even remotely resembling the young man was playing in the orchestra. Afterwards it was impossible to get a taxi. She had to wait in a long queue in the drenching rain. Water ran down her neck and dripped off her nose. If it required this mundane discomfort to bring her back to reality, here it was. After tonight she would be a sober, intelligent young American enjoying her trip abroad and absorbing with pleasure the new sights and sounds.

Her eyes would not seek for only one head in the crowd.

The queue moved and jostled as a bus drew up. Claudia was pushed forward and literally propelled on board. She had grown much more agile about buses now, and sprang up the stairs nimbly. The young man behind her did the same, and squeezed with a sigh of relief into the seat beside her.

It was against every law of averages that there could have been a repeat scene on a bus. But there was. The young man beside her mopping his wet hair was *him*.

Claudia sat absolutely rigid for two stops. Then, terrified that he would get off without having noticed her or spoken, she said, "Thanks for explaining your money system that day. I really have it worked out now."

The young man turned sharply, "Miss America!"

Off guard with surprise, there was no doubting the pleasure in his face. Claudia's heart did a quick flip-flop.

"I'm not Miss America, you know. I'm just a working girl. It's my aunt who insisted on staying at the Dorchester." As his eyebrows raised in their beautiful puzzled curve, she went on, "I've been doing the concerts. I've been every night this week. Where's your violin?"

"I wasn't playing tonight. I just wanted to hear Karajan conducting. I say, you know, I've been thinking about you. I thought you were the prettiest——" He stopped and blushed. He was shy, like nearly all Englishmen, and utterly wonderful.

"Do you have to rush back now to your aunt? Could we stop somewhere for coffee? My name's James Raymond."

"Mine's Claudia Browne. Yes, do let's stop. Anyway, I love catching buses. I love everything about London."

They had scrambled down the stairs again and were in the driving rain. Claudia clung to his arm, laughing. "Even the rain. It's romantic, somehow. My aunt was shocked when I told her I'd talked to a strange man on a bus, but she'd do the same thing on a ship and think it was correct. Isn't this fun meeting again?"

He was looking down at her with his bright, humorous gaze. "These things happen in London, strangely enough. Thank heaven for London. You didn't tell me you liked music."

"Oh, I *do*! Anyway, we were too deeply concerned with money the other day when we met. And you thought I was a millionaire, when actually I have to earn my living the same as anyone else. I work in an art gallery. And you?"

"I play second violin," James replied. "But next week I'm to play first in Glasgow," he went on, the deliberately casual voice giving away his pride. "It's quite an opportunity."

"Oh, I'm sure it is. What's Glasgow like?"

"Dreary and gray and Scottish. One doesn't go there from a choice."

"Sounds nice," Claudia murmured.

"Let's go in here for coffee. At least it will be dry. Glasgow isn't nice at all, but with me it's always the people who count more than the place."

"Oh, I do agree. If the right people are there. What an adorable place this is!"

"It's rather fun, isn't it? London's full of these places. Take your coat off, it's dripping."

"Yes. So's yours!"

They were laughing at each other. It was as if they had

known one another long enough to be utterly comfortable, yet not too long for the meeting not to be fraught with excitement and interest.

"Is there somewhere to hang them?" asked Claudia, standing in the so-simple, so-expensive black chiffon dress which she had forgotten she was wearing.

James noticed it at once. His gaze went from the tip of her well-groomed head, to her feet in the high-heeled evening shoes that were quite unsuitable for catching buses on a wet night. He said nothing. But the withdrawn look that came over his face said everything. He didn't believe a word of her story about being a working girl. Perhaps she was traveling with her aunt. But obviously the money was there. Overwhelming pots of it. And he was a courteous, sensitive young man who played second violin in an orchestra.

Claudia wanted to burst out with the whole story. The mining shares that had suddenly soared, Aunt Adelaide's dream about dressing and grooming her for a shipboard romance, the shaming fact that at home she had been too serious and studious and critical to have any beaux. . . .

But the young, wary face opposite her prevented all this. He wouldn't believe a word anyway. He had decided by now that she was a rich, bored American looking for sensations, man-hungry—oh, how awful!

Claudia's mind froze. She tried to make conversation, but it was stilted. "Have you always wanted to be a musician?"

"Always. My family expected me to do law. My father's a barrister. But I was determined to play the violin, even though there's no money—well, not yet. Perhaps some day. . . ."

"What's wrong?" said Claudia fiercely.

But his eyes had gone back speculatively to her charming dress. And it was no use. Not tonight, at least. The mood had gone. It could not be recaptured.

"I'd better go," she said at last. "I think if it's still raining I'll take a taxi."

"I'll get you one. The Dorchester?"

"Yes. If I could drop you . . . ?"

"I live at Hampstead. I'll take the tube. It's been nice meeting you again, Miss Am—Miss Browne."

"Claudia," said Claudia miserably. "I hope your Glasgow concert is an enormous success."

"Thank you," he said bleakly. "If you're going to the Albert Hall again you might make a point of hearing the Beethoven Fifth."

"I won't be. My thing is pictures."

"Ah. I see."

So now, thought Claudia furiously, I'm being sent off home with a couple of French Impressionists each worth a small fortune. That unutterably stupid English moron!

"Claudia, dear," said Aunt Adelaide worriedly, "don't you want to go to any more concerts?"

"No thank you, Aunt Adelaide."

"Not even the opera at Covent Garden?"

"Opera!"

"But I thought you had developed this passion for music."

"Not for music. Only for . . . but it's no use. He's going to Glasgow next week."

"He! Claudia, not this extraordinary young man you

met on that bus! You don't mean you've been seeing him
all the time?"

"I've not been seeing him at all," Claudia declared
passionately. "Or scarcely at all."

"Oh, goodness me! But didn't I tell you buses were
so ephemeral. You can't make serious friendships on
them."

"No, Aunt Adelaide."

Aunt Adelaide looked at her wan face and was dis-
tressed.

"Now, honey, let's go out and buy a fabulous dress."

Claudia spun round, "Don't mention dresses to me,
Aunt Adelaide! Not ever again!"

If only she had explained seriously to James last night
the true position he would have believed her. Why hadn't
she been able to? Because they were so new to one
another, so sensitive, so eager, that the smallest misunderstanding became an impenetrable barrier. It was her fault
that the misunderstanding had happened. It had been
within her power to remove it. But, shut behind her shyness and her desperate longing, she had not been able
to. It was so absurd to admit that she had fallen in love
at first sight. It just didn't happen, or, according to Aunt
Adelaide, only on ships.

And now everything was too late. She would never find
him again.

"Ruth," said Aunt Adelaide, "I'm worried about Claudia. She's moping. Really moping."

"I've noticed that, Addie. Just as if she's in love."

"She is in love, believe it or not, with that absurd young
man she met on a bus! He plays in an orchestra. He's
going to Glasgow, or somewhere equally awful."

"Glasgow's not the end of the world."

"It might as well be. Heavens, if only that silly girl had done this on a ship, there she has the man trapped, unless he jumps overboard. But all this business of buses and trains doesn't seem quite respectable."

"Trains?" said Aunt Ruth.

"What else is there for it? We must move with the times. And he's the only man the child's shown the slightest interest in. So there it is. Instead of that Dior dress it will have to be a return ticket to Glasgow. Though the saving will be considerable. You know, Ruth, we might have a little fling ourselves on the balance. We're not that old! Some good clothes, and the sea journey home. . . ."

Aunt Adelaide's eyes took on an anticipatory gleam.

Aunt Ruth said practically, "Have you told Claudia?"

"No. I'm going to now. I've discovered there are two very good Rembrandts in the Glasgow art gallery. She ought to see them."

Claudia said good-bye to them at King's Cross. She wore her raincoat over a sensible budget-priced tweed suit that she had bought the day before, out of her own money. Her cheeks were bright, her eyes as blue as the misty Hebridean sky.

"I don't know why I've agreed to go," she said.

"To see the Rembrandts, of course," said Aunt Adelaide firmly. "If other things fail they'll be there."

"Other things won't fail," said Claudia, just as firmly.

Then she realized she had given herself away, and her cheeks deepened to an even more beguiling pink. She could scarcely wait to walk casually through the train. The journey took all day. There was heaps of time to get misunderstandings straightened out. And maybe later, in Glasgow, she would see the Rembrandts as well!

The train began to move.

She leaned out calling happily, "Thank you, *darling* Aunt Adelaide!"

The two sisters were left on the platform. Aunt Adelaide shrugged. "Well, as you always say, Ruth, 'to travel hopefully is better than to arrive'."

"But this time she will arrive," said Ruth with conviction. She linked her arm with her sister's. "Just as we did!"

# Love in the Wilderness

When at last her Aunt Mabel died, everyone thought Lavinia would marry Harold Easterhill.

However, she did not do this. She collected her legacy of five hundred pounds, small enough, to be sure, but sufficient to put into a little business of some kind, and announced that she was going to London.

In response to all the alarmed twitters, she smiled placidly and said that she had always wanted to go to London. She had been delayed for ten years, first through nursing her Uncle Thomas, and then her Aunt Mabel, and now she was thirty-one, but it still wasn't too late. She had her legacy, and that would see her through until she got a job. True, she wasn't trained for anything, not

even nursing, although her elderly relatives had gladly
enough made do with her amateur talents. But she would
find something.

On the surface it would seem that she had no particular
assets, except her shining optimism, to take to London.

She was small and square, with a little, earnest, innocent pug face. In her Aunt Mabel's beaver lamb coat
she was even more square, which, in a way, was re-
assuring to Harold, as it meant she wasn't likely to attract men by her looks. As for her money, that was
little enough, too, and she would really be quite safe
while she went through the daunting experience of finding
that big cities were not for the likes of her.

Harold knew she would come back, but, alas, she was
not likely to come back with her five hundred pounds
intact—which was a great pity, as that, combined with
his own savings, really could have started a nice little
business.

However, there it was. Unexpectedly stubborn, as broad
as a hibernating bear in her beaver lamb coat, hope and
faith shining in her earnest blue eyes, Lavinia set out for
London. She promised to write as soon as she had a
permanent address.

This she found almost at once. It was the realization
of the first of her dreams, a place of her own, humble
certainly (it was a basement room with minute kitchen
and bathroom, and acquiring its lease cost her four-fifths
of her capital) but really her own.

She looked round the four walls and thought happily
what a pot of paint and some bright colors would do.
The furniture, which had been included in the lease, was
serviceable but quite ugly. It would be possible, however,

to find, in second-hand shops and markets, some more interesting things.

This was when Lavinia realized the second of her dreams.

For some reason unknown to her (perhaps she had seen illustrations in a fairy-story book, perhaps in some other life she had been a princess, she imagined fancifully) she had always longed to have a white velvet couch. It had seemed to her a most beautiful attainment, like writing a poem or growing a black rose, or taming a peacock, the kind of thing that brought color and luxury into life, that lifted it above nursing elderly relations and living in basement rooms, and even marrying dull, good men like Harold Easterhill.

A white velvet couch with tightly sunk buttons in its quilted back, and one flaunting scarlet cushion.

She found the couch in the Portobello Road market, a shabby thing with its horsehair insides drearily trailing out of its faded repp cover. It cost her three pounds. To have it covered in white velvet (a very impractical color, the upholsterer told her disapprovingly) would cost another twenty-one pounds.

It was a very cheap price for the attainment of a dream.

Lavinia, in a placid voice that belied the sparkle in her eyes, told the man to go ahead and do the work as quickly as possible.

She then had about thirty-five pounds left in her bank account. She would have to start looking for a job.

The woman in the employment agency at which she called was not enthusiastic.

"If you don't want to be a companion or a nanny——"

"No," said Lavinia firmly, "neither of those."

"And you say you can't do typing or keep books."

"I'm sorry. I was never taught."

"Then I'm afraid there's only one thing we can offer you at the moment, dear, and that's a selling position."

"Behind a counter?" Lavinia asked nervously.

"No, it's a house-to-house thing. Or office-to-office, if you like. To persuade people, business men mostly, to become members of Haute Cuisine Club. It costs five guineas a year and you get a discount on your bill if you eat at certain restaurants."

"Oh," said Lavinia. "Am I the person to do that?"

Frankly no, thought the woman. Although the funny little creature seemed completely honest. At least she wasn't the kind who would get doors slammed in her face. And this job was going begging.

"You could try, couldn't you, dear? Two pounds a week and commission on the number of members you get. Try to catch business men leaving their offices—you won't get to see them by asking their secretaries—and call at houses in good neighborhoods. I'm sure you'll do very well."

"All right," said Lavinia, screwing up her courage. "I'll try."

Because at least it meant she could make her own hours of work, and that meant that among other things she could be home when the couch was delivered.

Actually she did better than she had expected. Some people, liking her earnest little face, gave her cups of tea and nobody rudely rebuffed her. In the first week she had earned two pounds commission, and she hoped, with experience, to do very much better.

And she was able to wait in, in delicious expectation, the morning the couch was due to arrive.

The men came down the basement steps, carrying it uncovered, in all its pristine glory, at precisely the time they were expected.

She opened the door wide to let them in, one, two, three of them, though the third, a very large, strong and untidy man, seemed to be leaving all the work to the other two.

She fluttered about telling them exactly where to put the couch in the space that had stood ready for days. They dumped it down.

"There you are, miss. Nice piece of furniture. Grand-looking, though you'll have to be careful not to spill things on it. Well, good day, miss."

They tramped back up the steps, and Lavinia stood in a trance gazing at the beautiful object, so snow-white, so magnificent. Those lovely buttons pursed into little crevices, that silky pile. . . .

"Do you mind telling me," said a voice behind her, "why you wanted a piece of furniture like this?"

Lavinia spun round. She thought the men had gone, but the third one was still there.

He stood, enormously large, his head almost touching the low ceiling. His tweed coat was sagging, his trousers unpressed. He had untidy faded blond hair and very blue pondering eyes. His features were rather formless, a bulbous nose, heavy jowls, thick tufted eyebrows.

"I like it," she said, not questioning his presence, but glad someone had stayed to share her excitement. "I've always wanted it."

"Exactly like that?"

"More or less. That high back, certainly, because it has plenty of space for the buttons. I love the buttons. It has to have a scarlet cushion, of course. Oh, I know what you're thinking," she added, "that it doesn't really fit into this room, or even into my sort of life."

The man smiled suddenly, a wide grin that lifted his heavy jowls and made his face deeply understanding and tender. It was a very moving smile.

"Magnificences always fit in. People should have them —like jeweled stomachers and splendid nuptial beds. You're a very wise woman, Miss——"

"Miss Ashton. Lavinia Ashton. But didn't you know me?"

"Hadn't a clue. I just followed those workmen in."

"You just followed them!"

"I couldn't resist seeing what someone was going to do with such a magnificent thing as a white velvet couch in a basement room. Forgive me, Miss Ashton."

"Oh, don't ask me to forgive you," Lavinia cried.

The thick eyebrows rose. "Why not?"

"You're not that sort of person, are you? Expecting to be forgiven."

A flicker of startled appreciation crossed his face.

"No, I'm not. I'm even going to be impertinent enough to write a story about this for my paper."

"Oh! You're a reporter!"

"Cornelius Peterson. May I write the story?"

"Why, of course. If you think anyone will be interested."

"They'll be interested. A bit of human faith in this wilderness. Now, what about putting the kettle on, and telling me a few things about yourself?"

There was little enough to tell, but this man with the intent eyes didn't seem to find her story either dull or ordinary. He drank two cups of tea, nodded vehemently now and again, made one or two perspicacious comments, and finally, with another long, thoughtful stare at the couch that unashamedly embellished the room, like a carnation in a tramp's buttonhole, left her.

By that time she was in a complete flutter. She did not know in which newspaper the story would appear, nor did it greatly matter. What did matter was that she, Lavinia Ashton, thirty-one and plain of face and form, had already made her small private impact on the world. It justified everything she had done.

But Harold Easterhill did not look at it that way. He visited her the next day and disapproved suspiciously of everything, but, most of all of the couch.

"How much did you pay for that thing?" he demanded.

"Twenty-four pounds," she told him, since she was invariably honest.

"Are you mad? Under that fancy cover it's most likely stuffed with horsehair."

"It is," Lavinia admitted.

"It'll show every mark. Any sort of velvet is hard to clean, but *white* velvet!" He looked at her in complete incomprehension. "What's happened to you, Vinnie? I always thought you were a sensible girl."

"But you never knew me, Harold. Did you?" Lavinia said steadily.

He shook his head slowly and rather angrily, and suddenly, with her kind heart, she was sorry for him. Harold's requirements of life did not include magnificences. He just didn't understand them.

"Do sit down, Harold. I've made some coffee. Sit on the couch. It's very comfortable, you'll see."

He sat gingerly on the edge. He continued to protest angrily about the way she was choosing to live, and hinted darkly as to where it was likely to lead her. But when, in mild justification of her behavior she told him about Cornelius Peterson and the piece that had been in the paper, he got so perturbed that he moved his hands violently and upset his coffee on the couch.

"Oh!" Lavinia cried in distress. As the stain widened fatally she lost her temper. "Harold Easterhill, you clumsy fool! You've always stood on my dreams!"

"I'm sorry, Vinnie," he said ashamedly.

"Oh, it's no use being sorry. It's done. It's the end. I don't want to see you any more. I never have loved you and you haven't loved me. So it's better that we part."

Then he became angry, too. He stood up, shaking his head warningly.

"Lavinia, I don't know what will become of you. You're not so young any more——"

"Young enough to know there are still things like sunsets and peacocks, and—and—nuptial beds," she finished defiantly.

He was completely shocked.

"If that's the way your mind's working, Vinnie, then I think we had better part. You're not the girl I knew. You've got your head filled already with dangerous nonsense."

"Oh, go away!" Lavinia said crossly. "I want to get this stain out of the couch before it settles."

When he had gone she felt nothing but relief. Her life stretched ahead of her in glorious uncertainty, and never again were any of her cherished things going to be spoiled by his heavy hand. She rubbed away at the brown stain, and when it seemed inevitable that always a faint mark would remain, she told herself blithely that that would serve as a happy reminder of what she had escaped.

After that she decided that she had better go out on her job, as now she was utterly dependent on her own efforts.

She decided to start with the houses in the square immediately adjoining her street. This was a wealthy and well-cared-for square with roses climbing up the fronts of the houses, and smartly painted front doors, and colorful window-boxes. Lavinia marched up the path to the first door and rang the bell optimistically.

After quite a long time there were slow shuffling footsteps and the door was opened. Cornelius Peterson, the very large blond man, more untidy than ever, in a loose velvet jacket and sagging tie, stood there.

"Miss Ashton!" he said, in surprise.

Lavinia was overcome with embarrassment.

"Oh, I'm sorry. I didn't know you lived here, Mr. Peterson. I wouldn't have bothered you."

"Bothered me! How? Is that your job, going about bothering people? You didn't tell me that yesterday."

"Oh, well, you see, I sell things," she explained uneasily.

"What things?" It was impossible to escape that highly inquisitive gaze.

"Well, membership to a food club, actually. You get

reductions at certain restaurants. Good restaurants. *Haute cuisine.*"

"What do you know about *haute cuisine?*"

"Nothing, really. But that doesn't matter, so long as I can persuade people to join. Only believe me, I didn't mean to trouble you."

"Why not? I troubled you by walking uninvited into your house yesterday. Of course I'll join your club."

"Oh, will you really?" Lavinia cried.

He shook his thick forefinger at her.

"You know something, young lady? You're going to be a success at this job."

"Do you think so?"

"If you look like that, you're going to charm larks down out of the high blue sky. And not to be consumed by gourmets, either. But it seems to me, if you're going to talk food to people, you ought to know more about it. Lunch with me tomorrow. I'll take you to a place where the food really is out of this world."

"Lunch? Well——"

"Now why are you looking so worried? I'm thirty-eight, I haven't got a wife, I'm lazy and degenerate, but I behave fairly respectably at lunch times."

"It's just—what would I wear?" Lavinia said with her usual honesty.

The blue intense gaze beneath the thick, untidy brows bored into her.

"Have you ever worried before what clothes you would wear?"

"No. I don't believe I have."

"Then it's too late to begin now. Just wear that charming, optimistic little face."

It was true that it didn't matter what she wore, for in the low-ceilinged, rather dark restaurant she was gathered into the welcome that was accorded to her host. She was a person of taste and importance because she was accompanied by this large, vaguely shambling, carelessly dressed, benevolent man.

Cornelius introduced her to the head waiter.

"Miss Ashton is up from the country and we have to show her what London food can be. So, Pierre, if you let me down, I'll slit your throat."

The dark-faced Pierre smiled as if the thought of having his throat slit by Mr. Peterson would be the height of joy.

"May I suggest some *Bisque de Homard*, sir, followed by *boeuf à la mode*? Or perhaps you would care to begin with oysters?"

"This is a serious business," said Cornelius. "Bring us two dry Martinis and we'll reflect."

Lavinia, needless to say, was not accustomed to Martinis at lunch, or indeed at any other time. Nor had she imagined food could be so poetic a business. She was entranced. Her cheeks flushed a camellia pink and her eyes shining, she ate and talked and sipped her wine and lost most of her inhibitions.

"Isn't the world an exciting place?" she said, and the statement didn't seem trite. It was both profound and true.

"It's a wilderness," Cornelius said, sombrely. "That's why it's good to find someone with a little faith in it. Even if expressed in strange ways."

Lavinia looked at him ruefully. "Harold spilt coffee on my couch."

"Harold? You didn't tell me about Harold yesterday."

"I didn't tell you everything," Lavinia said severely.

"So I see." His heavy jowls seemed heavier. "So Harold didn't approve of the magnificence."

"Oh, he didn't spill the coffee deliberately. No," she added honestly, "he didn't approve. He thought I was crazy. Do you think I'm crazy, Cornelius?"

"In the nicest way." He studied her in his assessing way, to which she was now growing accustomed and even growing to like. "You have a delightful little pansy face. Even without Harold, you'll do very well. You have imagination and courage. You think things are nice when they aren't, which is a charming characteristic. Waiters, as you can see, enjoy serving you. That, also, is a characteristic to be desired. Oh, yes, my dear, you'll do very well."

"Thank you," said Lavinia gratefully. "So, I'm sure, will you."

"Tell me," he prompted.

The wine had made her bold.

"Well, you won't always be just a hack reporter, looking for stories about insignificant people like me. You'll have things offered to you, being a foreign correspondent, probably, or some other important assignment."

"What makes you think that?" He was interested. His jowls were lifted by his faint, tender smile, his eyes missed nothing.

"To me you're that kind of person."

"Thank you, Lavinia," he said, with humility. "Thank you."

And then the woman came sweeping up to them. She wore a black dress, and a hat that was simply a full-blown dark red rose. There were jewels in her ears, Lavinia knew intuitively, that were diamonds.

"Cornelius, darling! How wonderful to see you. I thought you were in one of your hibernating moods."

"So I am," Cornelius growled. His face, once again, looked heavy and lugubrious. "But one has to eat, even then. Lavinia, this is the Baroness von Lindenburgh. Miss Ashton, Elena. You're not here alone, I take it?"

"No. Timothy's over there. I had to come and have a word with you. How are the newspapers?"

"All right," Cornelius said briefly.

The woman's brilliant eyes flickered to Lavinia.

"Cornelius treats his newspapers as if they were his children. He should really try the real thing, shouldn't he? We've been trying to persuade him for years."

She fluttered her hand at them and walked away, leaving a faint, delicious flower scent behind her.

"That was Elena von Lindenburgh," Cornelius said unnecessarily.

"Yes. You told me. She's beautiful, isn't she?" All of Lavinia's shyness and inhibitions had come back. She was a countrywoman in a shabby tweed suit, sitting in an expensive restaurant where she didn't belong, with a complete stranger. Far more complete than she had imagined.

"Is she?"

"I thought so."

Cornelius beckoned the waiter and asked for the bill. His brows were lowering, his face sunk in forbidding lines.

"Mr. Peterson?"

"You were calling me Cornelius five minutes ago."

"Was I? I didn't mean to."

"Why, in heaven's name, not?" he asked savagely. "Because five minutes ago you didn't know I owned four newspapers. It doesn't alter my name."

"Are you—very wealthy?" she asked timidly.

"More than is good for me. Yes." He looked at his watch.

"Oh, you have to go?"

"I'm afraid so. I've a board meeting. I'll put you in a taxi."

The efficient doorman got a taxi in a regretfully short time. Lavinia, sad from too much wine or too much food, or just too much of a world that wasn't so full of joy, after all, climbed in.

"Thank you so much for the *lovely* food," she said in a voice that sounded unlike her own, that could almost have belonged to the Baroness von Lindenburgh.

"That's all right," he said. "Glad you liked it. Hope it's given you a talking point."

His voice was gruff. His eyes, beneath the tufted brows, were curiously stony. He had grown in authority. He was, all at once in spite of his careless appearance, a newspaper magnate. And she was an insignificant mouse from the country. How very absurd and unlikely the whole thing was.

Lavinia called at the employment agency the next day.

"Who is Cornelius Peterson?" she asked the woman in charge.

"I'm sure I don't know, dear. There's only one person I know of that name, and I don't suppose it's likely to be him. He owns a fleet of newspapers."

"It is him," Lavinia said bleakly. "He's joined the club."

"Oh, splendid! You are doing well, dear."

"Am I?" said Lavinia.

"It must be that innocent, trusting expression you have. I don't suppose you know a thing about *haute cuisine*, really, do you?"

"Not very much," Lavinia admitted. "But a little." Her pride asserted itself. "Yes, I do know a little."

But from then on she avoided going into the square where Cornelius Peterson lived. Indeed, she looked cautiously out of her front door before she set out at all, in case she should embarrass him by encountering him. He had been kind to a very naïve and unworldly woman from the country, partly because she had provoked his passing interest, and partly because he was naturally kind. That was all. Now he would have gone back to his habitual circle of friends which included people like the beautiful Baroness. He was wealthy enough to be untidy and eccentric, and even rude, as he no doubt frequently was. But he wasn't likely to spare many more thoughts for his very brief acquaintance with Lavinia Ashton. He had given her a kind word in passing, and now she was on her own.

She still had the white velvet couch, it was true, and she could, had they occurred to her, indulge in other (but inexpensive) magnificences for there was no one to stop her, or even laugh at her. Not even Harold.

But she had temporarily lost interest in inanimate objects. Her mind was filled with a human one, a large shambling man with a lugubrious face that lighted only infrequently to a rare and tender smile. Cornelius Peter-

son. She could not have him, but now no one else would
do.

Autumn slipped by into winter. The Haute Cuisine Club
eventually almost succeeded in starving its advocate. There
were not enough people interested or who could afford it.
In spite of her initial success, Lavinia at last had to admit
failure, and to take a dull but safe job selling nylons in
a big store. Life in London was not so amusing, after
all. The winter soot marked the white velvet couch and
it, like her life, began to seem tarnished and tired. Stuffed
with horsehair, after all. Harold had been right.

Too shy to make many friends, she was rather lonely
in those weeks. Her closest friend was Miss Tidworth from
the floor above her. She had discovered that Miss Tidworth owned a cat which she doted on, and was reluctant
to leave too long alone. Poor Charley hated his own
company, she said.

So Lavinia offered to spend the evenings when Miss
Tidworth had to go to her job at the local library, in her
flat with Charley. He was a sulky, unfriendly cat and did
not take to Lavinia. They spent most of the evening glar-
ing at one another from opposite chairs. It was scarcely
companionship from either's point of view, but when
Miss Tidworth came home she made cocoa, and they
had long pleasant chats over the gas fire.

Miss Tidworth had been to visit at Lavinia's, too, and
had seen the couch. But her only comment had been,
"I think I'd rather have had a fridge, dear. So much more
practical. Oh, look, you've gone and spilt something on
it."

"That was Harold."

"Harold!" Miss Tidworth's eyes sparkled with interest.

"You didn't tell me you had a boyfriend."

"I haven't really. Not now. Actually, it was the couch we quarrelled over."

"Frankly, I'm not surprised, dear. I expect he thought you were getting ideas above your station in life."

Miss Tidworth looked at Lavinia kindly, seeing her plain, flat little face, her stocky figure, her uninspired clothes which always seemed to make her look broader and shorter than necessary. No one, her expression said, would be likely to want to marry such an unexciting little person, especially if she had foolish extravagances. Miss Tidworth's world was purely practical.

Lavinia, shedding a few ashamed tears into her pillow that night, decided that in future hers must be, also. A world of fifteen- and thirty-denier nylons and the varying shapes of women's legs, of crowded buses and eating starchy canteen lunches that tended to add to her rotundity, of week-ends spent visiting museums and taking long walks across the park, and sometimes exchanging a few words with dreary-looking people in teashops. A practical world that was a wild, sad wilderness.

The day after shedding those ashamed tears was a Sunday. It was very cold and beginning to snow. Rather than stay in her flat and risk brooding, a habit her cheerful nature rebelled against, Lavinia decided to take a long bus ride. She climbed to the upper deck of the first bus that came along, and found that one of the front seats was empty. She had settled herself contentedly in it before she realized that the large overcoated man in the opposite one was Cornelius Peterson.

It didn't seem likely that a millionaire would ride, from

choice, in a bus, but there he was, and before she could hastily exchange her seat he had seen her.

His face lighted up. (But it had done that for the Baroness, too. He was a courteous man.)

"Lavinia!" he exclaimed, and promptly moved across to share her seat.

It was a fairly tight fit, since neither of them was small, but Lavinia, squeezed against the snow-flecked window, immediately felt warm and snug, as if she were wrapped in furs and tenderness.

"Well, well, Lavinia. It's been a long time."

"Yes, it has, I suppose."

"No suppose about it. It's been a long time. I've been in the States, and—well, much busier than a congenitally lazy person like myself enjoys. What have you been doing? How's that food club thing?"

"Oh, I had to give that up. I'm selling nylons now."

He searched her face with the familiar attentive interest, as if he really cared what she was doing or how she felt about it. But she knew him better now. He had the kind of mind that dissected people's feelings and then casually flung them away.

"Do you like that, Lavinia? No, of course you don't. You loathe it."

"Oh, I'll find something more interesting later. I have to get some experience first."

He still studied her face, this time without speaking. Then he said, "Where are you going now? Just for a ride, like me?"

"Is that what you're doing, Mr. Peterson? Bus riding, for pleasure."

"Any law against it? Let's have tea at the terminus and

come back by a different route."

Lavinia's heart was bouncing madly. She tried to remain calm and prim, but she knew the pink of excitement was already in her cheeks.

"Thank you, Mr. Peterson. That would be nice."

"Come off it, Lavinia. It was Cornelius the last time we met."

They found a tea-shop at the terminus, but it was a dreary suburban area, and the buns beneath the glass-topped counter, the plastic-topped tables and the practical cups and saucers, all too familiar to Lavinia, were not Cornelius' usual fare.

He acted, however, as if he went into cafés every day of his life. He helped Lavinia off with her beaver lamb coat, took off his own coat, then sat opposite her, his face wearing a look of beaming excitement, as if he were on a picnic.

"Toasted crumpets, I think," he said. "How very pleasant meeting someone to have tea with me."

"Me, too," Lavinia murmured.

"You don't often do this? You've found no one to replace Harold?"

"Fancy you remembering about him! No, there's no one else. I'm thirty-one now."

"And so?"

He shouldn't ask her so many questions. He wasn't really interested. He couldn't be.

"Well, you have to have other things to make up for —for youth, I suppose."

"Beauty is in the eye of the beholder, Lavinia. A very old saying. But true."

Yes, it was true. For he, in his shabby velvet jacket,

with his tie too loosely knotted, his heavy jowls hanging
a little over his collar, his face deeply, earnestly creased,
his thick, tangled eyebrows raised quizzically, was entirely beautiful.

Lavinia's cheeks grew pinker and her hand was a
little unsteady as she poured the tea. She was blissfully
happy, but with an ache at the bottom of her happiness,
that, like a bandit, was going to spring on her when she
was alone.

"Then how's that superb extravagance of yours? The
couch."

"Oh, it's not very practical. My neighbor tells me I
should have bought a fridge. I suppose I should have,
too."

"So you're being practical now. You've no more magnificences."

"My wages don't really allow for them," she said steadily. She caught his anxious and probing gaze. "But one
day soon——" Suddenly, for no reason, optimism was
soaring in her. "Yes, I will buy another."

His eyes brightened. His extraordinary smile, sweet
and tender and embracing, spread over his heavy face.
For a moment he laid his hand over hers in an approving
caress.

"Good girl, Lavinia. I'd have been enormously disappointed if you'd let the nylons get you down."


When they left for home the snow had thickened, and
they sat on the top of the bus looking down on a suddenly white world. The dark, sooty roof-tops, the black-
ened tree trunks, the shabby and deserted streets were
sparkling and pure.

Her radiant mood lingering, Lavinia thought the whole world was like her white velvet couch. She found herself leaning slightly against Cornelius' shoulder. She didn't talk, and neither did he. They were two people isolated for a little while in a dream. But the dream was their only point of contact, for when they arrived at their destination and Lavinia said diffidently:

"You wouldn't—I suppose you couldn't spare time— I've a bottle of sherry———" His face was set back in its lugubrious lines.

"I'm terribly sorry. I've a dinner party. I'm late already. My housekeeper will be in a flap, as usual. I wonder she ever stays with me. I'm so sorry, Lavinia. But this has been wonderful. I'll be looking for you again on buses going south." His tender, sad eyes explored her face.

"Yes, of course," she said in her steady voice. "Anyway, I have to hurry, too. I'm looking after Charley tonight."

"Charley?"

"Oh, he's my neighbor's cat. We don't really like one another very much, but I think he's got a better nature than one would suppose on first acquaintance."

"Bless you, Lavinia!" said Cornelius suddenly, roughly, and was gone.

Lavinia had lied. She wasn't really looking after Charley that evening, because Miss Tidworth was home. But it had seemed better to mention him than no one at all, especially after what Cornelius had said about the dinner party, with the beautiful Baroness, most likely, and other glamorous people.

To her shame, when it was completely dark, she crept

out and walked along the snow-crisp pavement into the
square to look at his house, to see if the be-furred guests
were arriving or if, perhaps, the housekeeper who got
in a flap hadn't drawn the curtains.

But apart from a Rolls-Royce at the gate, and a chink
of light from one window, she could see and hear nothing.
She was just someone shut outside, an anonymous little
woman, too square in her beaver coat, too unpractical
and too innocent for the freezing wilderness she lived in.

For the rest of the winter Lavinia took bus rides on
Sunday afternoons whenever possible, but she didn't see
Cornelius again. She was moved from the stockings to the
glove counter in the shop, and got a raise of ten shillings
a week. Charley, at last, deigned to treat her with friend-
liness, and on her last visit had actually sprung on her
knee and settled down with a vibrating purr. Crocuses
were coming up in the parks, and optimism was springing
in her heart.

She bought a new coat and put the heavy beaver
away until next winter. She even plucked up courage to
go walking, in broad daylight, in the square which she
privately called "Mr. Peterson's." Not that it mattered
whether it were daylight or dark, for she never encountered him.

Until that awful, terrible spring evening when she didn't
see Cornelius himself, but the ambulance at his gate. It
was just moving away as she came into the square. For
one wild moment she told herself that it probably contained the housekeeper, the one who got in a flap. Then
she saw a woman going slowly back into the house, and
she knew it was not the housekeeper in the ambulance.
It was Cornelius.

She could not stop herself. She went hurrying up the bricked path after the woman, calling out:

"Please! Is Mr. Peterson ill?"

The woman turned. She was elderly and her face was splotched with tears.

"He's taken real bad, the poor man. He has to have an emergency operation."

"Oh, dear!" said Lavinia faintly. "Is it—very serious?"

"A ruptured appendix, the doctor thinks. Poor man! Poor dear man! And no one really to care. Oh, masses of friends, of course, but no one near and dear, so to speak. Who are you, if I may ask?"

"I'm—just a neighbor."

"In the square? I haven't seen you about."

"Round the corner. I know Mr. Peterson. Which hospital are they taking him to? I'll go and see him."

"The Westminster, dear. But don't go tonight. They wouldn't let you in. He'll be unconscious."

That lively, alert face unconscious! Oh, no. This woman just didn't know what she was talking about.

"I'll go in the morning," she said. "Even if they won't let me in they'll tell me how he is."


She went out as soon as the shops opened in the morning, and after careful thought selected a pot with six daffodils just coming into bloom. Then she set off for the hospital.

She had never been there before, and was bewildered by the vastness of it, but a receptionist told her which floor to go to, and a porter took her up in the lift.

There, in the long corridor, she waited until a nurse came hurrying by.

"Excuse me. Is Mr. Peterson on this floor?"

"In number seven. But he's not allowed visitors. Are you a relation?"

Lavinia shook her head.

"Then there's not a chance." The nurse was aware of Lavinia's distress and was briskly kind. "But he's a little better this morning. Do you want to leave those flowers?"

"Yes, please."

"I'll look after them for you."

She was already bustling away.

"May I wait?" Lavinia called after her.

"Goodness, no. That won't do any good. Run along home. Ring up later."

She counted the hours until two o'clock. Then she telephoned. A calm voice told her that the patient's slight improvement had been maintained. She remembered, all at once, that she was supposed to be at work. She reluctantly dropped more pennies in the slot and rang the shop to say a friend was seriously ill, and she wouldn't be at work for a day or two, perhaps a week. She knew she would lose her salary, but that couldn't be helped. She would manage. If need be, she could sell something. She spent the afternoon and evening nursing Charley, who had now rather taken to her, or at least to the comfort of her lap. She didn't eat. She didn't really do anything except listen to Charley's purr and her own thoughts.

The next day at the hospital they said he was stronger, but not yet out of danger, and the following day the news was much the same. On the fourth day, when she reached the required floor, she had a feeling of faintness, and sat on the bench at the end of the corridor. After a while she felt better, but continued to sit there because it was suddenly comforting just to feel she was near Cornelius. If she sat there unobstrusively they might let her stay for several hours.

This, however, was not to be, for presently the same nurse came along, smiling in a friendly way.

Lavinia sprang up guiltily.

"I was just resting a moment. How is Mr. Peterson?"

"You're the lady who brought the daffodils?"

"Yes."

"You didn't put a card in them. Mr. Peterson's been wondering who they were from. I had to describe you."

"Oh! How silly of me. I forgot the card."

"Never mind, he guessed who you were. He wants to see you."

"Me!"

"Yes. But only for a few minutes. You're his first visitor."

"Me!" said Lavinia again, incredulously.

She went into the room very quietly and crossing over to the bed she looked down on his face, not greatly changed except for its pallor and a deeper scoring of the lines. No one could see her madly racing heart, or guess the effort it was to say in a voice that didn't tremble:

"Hallo, Cornelius."

"Hallo, Lavinia. They told me you've been here every day. Why?"

She knew he wasn't to talk much. His brief question sounded curt and aggressive, as if he must get to the bottom of the matter with the minimum of effort. With those eyes probing into her, she had no choice but to be honest.

"I suppose it's because I love you," she said matter-of-factly.

She saw the faint consternation in his face before he closed his eyes. Then he simply looked tired and extinguished, the lively, alert, inquisitive Cornelius she knew hiding behind that locked face.

"But don't let it worry you," she said nervously. "I only told you because you asked me."

"Yes," he said at last. "I ask too many questions. Too damn many questions. So I deserve an answer like that. But I don't want it, do you understand?" His eyes flew open, disconcerting her with their brilliance.

"I didn't really expect you would." Lavinia looked round the room, which was full of the most expensive varieties of flowers. Some would be from women like the Baroness, from wealthy friends, perhaps even from rival newspaper magnates. Only the humble pot of daffodils was from a shop girl.

"The nurse said I mustn't stay," she went on in her calm, optimistic voice. "It was very kind of you to let me see you. I'm so glad you're getting better."

She began to move away.

"Lavinia, you've only seen me three times, or four, if you can count this travesty of myself."

"And there won't be a fifth if she doesn't go now," said the nurse, coming in.

Lavinia had an appalling and overwhelming desire to weep.

"I—I'll see you on a bus, perhaps," she said.

"Never! You've got to forget it, Lavinia. Forget it!"

She didn't go to the hospital the next day. What was the use? He didn't want to see her, and she would only weep, and that nurse was losing patience with her, anyway. She walked about the streets for several hours and then went home and nursed Charley. The following day, because she had no money to pay the rent, she got a second-hand furniture dealer to come and give her a price for the couch. He offered her five pounds.

"Is that all? But it cost three times that price to have it covered."

"Not a very practical color, Miss. And marked, too. It'll have to be cleaned."

"Oh! All right, then. I'll take five pounds."

The man sensed her distress, and gave her another pound. But even that spontaneous gesture did not disprove what Cornelius had said. The wilderness was all around her, and she didn't think she could fight it any longer.

Several days later she pulled herself together and went back to the shop. They had taken her off the glove counter and put her back on nylons, she discovered.

"Sorry, dear," the buyer told her briskly, "but you were very vague about how long you'd be away and gloves were busy."

"I understand," said Lavinia. "That's all right. At least, I didn't get the sack."

"Oh, no, we wouldn't do that if we could help it. Is your friend better?"

"Getting better, thank you."

"Well, then, cheer up, dear. The sale starts tomorrow. There's masses to do."

Because of the imminent sale, Lavinia worked later, and

when she got home it was almost dark. She climbed wearily down the steps to the basement door and let herself in.

A form, very large, head almost touching the ceiling, rose in front of her.


"Thought you were never coming home, Lavinia," said Cornelius. "Your friend upstairs, the one with the cat, let me in. What have you done with the couch?"

"Cornelius!" she whispered, standing stock still. "You're better?"

"I'm fine," he said impatiently. "Come now," he added, after a moment. "I'm not a ghost. Where's that couch?"

"Oh, I sold it. I got tired of it."

"*Tired* of it!"

Lavinia's eyes fell beneath his fierce regard.

"Well, I had to be practical."

"You mean you needed the money."

After a moment she said, "I only got six pounds for it. For all those lovely tight buttons."

"And what am I to sit on now?"

She collected herself.

"Oh, I'm so sorry." She pushed a chair forward. "I know my flat looks rather dreary without the couch." It had looked dreary, but it didn't at this moment, with him there, filling the room with his size and his vitality. "Are you really well, Cornelius?"

"Perfectly well." His tone told her not to fuss.

"I'm so glad."

"But you've got thinner."

"I've been walking a lot."

"At the shop?"

It was impossible to deceive him.

"I took a few days off."

"Why? Because of me? So you could hang around the hospital? Is that why you're short of money?"

Lavinia flushed, but she said steadily, "They don't pay wages if you're away, unless you can produce a doctor's certificate."

He looked at her with his probing, assessing gaze for a long time. Then at last he said, "Sorry I was so rough on you when you came to see me." He moved his hand towards her, then drew it back, and said aggressively, "I told you to forget this nonsense. Didn't I?"

"It's no use asking the impossible, Cornelius."

"But why? Why? I'm just someone who liked your gallant approach to things. It interested me. So I took you to lunch. I liked talking to you. But that was all. This shouldn't have happened, Lavinia."

He was being sorry for her. That was dreadful. Her lips quivered. She bit them fiercely. But at that moment she couldn't speak.

"I've got too much money," he was going on. "Far too much. I don't enjoy it, but I can't seem to help it. It's almost as much a disease as—well, arthritis, for instance, or dipsomania. I work too hard because I'm naturally lazy and I think I shouldn't be. So then I get bad-tempered and hate people most of the time. Most of them are worth hating, anyhow. I like being alone a lot and I particularly dislike small talk and insincere, vain women. I've never shone as an accomplished lover." His eyes brooded on her. "But the money is the biggest hurdle. You see, you get such tremendous fun living on a little and having moments of wild, enormously satisfying extravagance, buying your magnificences. There's the zest to your life. How would you be if it were taken away? If you could have everything you fancied? You wouldn't want any of it, Lavinia. That beautiful light of anticipation would go out of your face." He got up and came towards her. "Your charming little pug-dog face," he said, taking it in his hands. "All that would happen if you married me, Lavinia."

"M—married you!"

His brows drew together.

"For heavens' sake, what did you think this conversation was about?"

"I—couldn't believe that!" she whispered.

"You don't have to believe it. I told you to forget me. How would you be without any of your magnificences, your impractical, awkward, ill-fitting, wonderful, soul-satisfying magnificences? Now what——" He pondered over her in a puzzled way. "You have that look on your face that you had the day you showed me the couch."

"But don't you realize," said Lavinia softly, "*you* are my magnificence."

"Me! What! Awkward, ill-fitting, short-tempered, critical, illogical, lazy, untidy——"

"Soul-satisfying," she said, stopping his lips with her fingers.

And then at last the angry doubt eased out of his face, his heavy jowls lifted, his sweet moving smile embraced her.

"I love you, too, Lavinia," he said, as if he were finishing a conversation begun many days ago.

# *Mirage*

Set back a little from the street, with the sun pouring in its windows, the shop stood like a jewel in a shabby setting. On one side of it there was a drapery store hung to the doors with cheap and gaudy cottons, and presided over by a stout, flashing-eyed black woman with several children hopping like frogs about her; on the other, there was a fruit and vegetable market, odorous with the rich, warm smell of rotting bananas.

These mundane neighbors made Flora's Shop all the more unexpected, like a mirage. It had a path of cobblestones leading up to its yellow door, and a tree with feathery green leaves bent towards it. The door had a polished brass knocker shaped like a dragon, and above hung a swinging sign such as might hang from an inn, with "Flora's Shop" painted on it.

The windows themselves were astonishing. They contained a small but exciting collection of antiques. One might have been looking into the windows of a highly expensive Chelsea or Kensington art dealer's establishment.

And all this in such an unlikely spot, with the high warm Caribbean wind blowing, the sun beating down, the street jostling with gaudily dressed, slim-waisted, brown-faced girls and lounging, staring young men whose hair bore the sophisticated gleam of oil but whose eyes had still the round, rolling, inquisitive gaze of the children.

Anthony felt as if he had suddenly come upon order and civilization. That old highly polished rocking chair might have come out of his grandmother's parlour, the beautiful rosewood cabinet was exactly what he wanted for his flat in London. But more than that, the shawl, the ivory fan, the delicate and lovely porcelain figures suggested an irresistible feminine quality. He had an instinctive feeling that the owner of this shop, the mysterious Flora, would be as rare and beautiful as her wares. When he went in she would appear out of the darkness—as cool and pale as a water-lily—and smile at him.

Why did he suddenly have an overpowering instinct that in this out-of-way spot, the little Dutch town of Curaçao in the Caribbean, he would find his ideal of womanhood? He could not have said, but as he looked in the window it seemed to him, excitingly, that a face, fair and pale, glimmered in the gilt-rimmed mirror and was gone.

His hands were beginning to tremble with eagerness

and excitement as he turned the shining knob of the door. It refused to turn. The door must be locked.

Behind him Anthony heard a small "Oh!" of disappointment. He was startled, unaware that he had not been alone. He turned and saw the girl in the full-skirted pink cotton dress. She was hatless and her hair was so pale a shade as to be almost white. It framed her round young face in a curious purity.

"Is it shut?" she asked.

For a moment Anthony did not take in her question. He still had a vague resentment that his moment of privacy had been invaded.

"Yes, I'm afraid so," he said at last, trying the door handle again uselessly.

"Oh, dear! How disappointing! It looks such a heavenly shop. Surely it's too early to be closed for lunch? Oh, well!" The girl shrugged. "I shall have to come back later."

She strolled away and Anthony, except for still feeling that lingering resentment that she should have intruded into his dream, forgot her existence.

Presently he wandered off himself, and within the shop the dark hand that had been about to turn the handle of the door desisted. A look of bewilderment and disappointment lay over the woman's jolly brown face. She shook her tightly curled head slowly. The ways of white people were hard to understand, she thought. But those two would be back. As the day grew warmer and sleepier they would begin to behave like people who shared the same world. She knew. White people might be a little slower and more devious but they were the same in the end. A rich chuckle burst from deep inside the calico-covered bosom. Then she waddled off, for all her apparent clumsiness moving expertly among the carved chairs and tables and carefully displayed porcelain and glass.

"Was that a customer, Mina?" called a light, high voice from upstairs.

"No, ma'am. Not for us. Only they tourists passing."

"There's a big ship in today, Mina. Don't go to sleep."

"Sleep! Ma'am, you knows I never goes to sleep!"

Could it be that the dark young man really liked the graceful porcelain ladies better than the little pink and white, flesh and blood one who had stood beside him? Mina shook her head again, slowly and definitely. Her knowledgeable eyes shone with warmth and mischief. No, that just wasn't human nature.

For all the crowded noisy state of the town, with people jostling him off the narrow footpaths and shiny opulent cars driven by Dutch business men in light blue suits and gaudy ties, or by dusky-faced chauffeurs, flashing by, Anthony found himself deeply lonely. The market place with its piles of fruit and fish, tourists in large sun-hats, thin sneaking cats, tumbling children with enormous coquettish eyes, and their slow-footed majestic mammas, seemed to him vulgar and squalid. The gently rocking boats with their cargoes of fruit, manned by slim wrinkled sailors from Venezuela, at the edge of the canal, had no romance for him. He began to wish he had accepted the invitation of friends from the ship to spend the day ashore with them. Then he knew that his wish to explore alone had been guided by intuition. How could he have found Flora in her shop, slim and cool and exquisite, in company with several high-spirited travelers? In half an hour he would go back. If she had been having a morning coffee break he would by then have returned to the shop.

It was exasperating to a degree that when he returned to the small sunny cul-de-sac, Flora's Shop still remained closed and only the girl in the pink dress was there peering in the window.

She looked round at the sound of his footstep and said, "Oh! You again!" and returned to her study of the window.

"Is there no one here yet?" Anthony asked, deeply disappointed.

"No. As a matter of fact I thought I saw a shadow move inside just now, but I can't have. There's only furniture in there." She began to laugh, her cheeks dimpling. "Unless the place is haunted."

"It's like a mirage," Anthony said involuntarily. She turned to him, her face full of quick interest. "Do you know, that's what I thought, too. That shawl, that fan, that lovely mirror. They don't belong here, in all this heat and muddle. It's like—well, a beautifully dressed woman among a lot of fat, gaudy riffraff."

For the first time Anthony looked at the girl directly. Her lightly freckled face was round and young and pleasant, her lips were red, her eyes a bright blue. The pale-colored hair curled on her smooth forehead. She was like a white cat, he thought. Friendly as a cat, too. When she smiled at him her face dimpled. Suddenly, in a spontaneous way that rarely came to him, he was saying, "Haven't I seen you before?"

"You ought to have, I must say! We've been traveling on the same ship for three weeks."

"No! We haven't really?" Anthony's eyes were full of consternation.

The girl laughed again. "We have, you know. I've often seen you, but you've been—awfully remote."

"I've been working."

"Yes?" Her blue eyes sparkled with friendly interest.

"I write a little," said Anthony, and to his annoyance his voice sounded embarrassed.

"Oh, how clever! Do you sell things?"

"Not many. Some."

"Well!" Her obvious admiration was strangely pleasant. "Then of course you haven't had time for games and things."

"Actually—I'm not a very good mixer," Anthony heard himself saying, his shyness, always so carefully hidden behind a pose of aloofness and dignity, suddenly confessed. And to this scrap of a girl in a pink cotton dress! He couldn't believe his ears. What was happening to him? Was the warm, windy, Caribbean air getting into his blood, or was it his secret excitement about the cool, perfect woman who dwelt behind the closed doors of the shop?

"Look, why don't we go and eat somewhere?" he suggested with his new confidence. "When we come back this place must surely be open."

"Let's," said the girl gaily. "But wouldn't you like to know my name?"

"I should know it, I expect," Anthony said doubtfully.

"Oh, I don't see why you should. There are dozens of girls on the ship. I'm Diana Buckland, and I know you. You're Anthony Farmer. Actually I asked——Oh, quick! There's that awful Mrs. Read. If she sees us, we'll never escape."

Before he realized what was happenting, Anthony found himself grasped by the hand and being whisked into the fruit market next door. There, in the pungent odor of over-ripe fruit, still holding hands, they laughed with repressed hilarity, as Mrs. Read, the ship's stout, talkative menace, lumbered past.

"She's a terror," Diana whispered. "One night I couldn't escape from her for three hours. Hasn't she ever bothered you?"

"No."

"Oh, you're clever at evading people."

A soft Oriental voice behind them said, "Something you want, pliss?"

Anthony looked into the ingratiating face that had sprung into view behind the counter. It was like a fruit itself, wrinkled, lemon-colored, part of the warm odorous atmosphere, of the spell, growing over him.

"Let's have a pineapple," he said recklessly. "And what else? Mangoes, pawpaws, avocado pears?"

"We'll have to carry the things," Diana protested. But suddenly she was reckless too. "Let's buy some of everything. We can have a party on board tonight."

"A party?"

"Of course. It's time you stopped working and relaxed."

In the dim interior of Flora's Shop the huge black woman waddled to the windows and dropped the shutters. It was siesta time. She could now legitimately lock the door, no matter what plaintive complaint came from upstairs. She was nearly asleep already, yawning mightily.

Only fools and lovers stayed awake at noontime. Those two who had scampered off hand in hand would not sleep. They would be too busy discovering that flesh and blood were preferable to the cold perfection of porcelain. Ah, life was funny, the ways of the young even funnier. First they were blind to each other, then they found their tongues and talked and talked, then slowly their eyes changed, their tongues grew slower . . . .

Mina yawned again, chuckling sleepily. The shuttered noonday dusk hung over the polished Chippendale, the shining glass, and the icy limbs of the porcelain figures. But it could not extinguish the color of Mina's red dress, her ebony hair, and her gleaming copper skin. She lay relaxed on the fragile Empire couch, like a brilliant full-blown tropical lily.


Anthony had had the brilliant idea of hiring a car and going to the beach a few miles out of the town. They had swum in the turquoise pool safely netted from sharks, eaten watermelon with the juice dripping down their fingers, and then lain in the sun spread-eagled, drowsy with content.

Still in Anthony's mind, surrounded by its aura of delicious excitement, lay the picture of the shop, with Flora, unknown and mysterious, an exquisite jewel in its centre.

Diana was a remarkably attractive girl, he thought. She was slim and beautifully made, her limbs a smooth honey color that one had a secret desire to touch. Her face was laughing and full of life, her hair, tousled by the wind, charmingly babyish in its paleness and disarray. But she was not mysterious. She was disconcertingly easy to read.

Flora, the owner of that intriguing shop in the heart of

the sun-drowned town, was the unknown, the unattained.

"How did you happen to know my name?" Anthony asked lazily.

Diana scratched with a twig in the sand. "I found out," she said.

"Why?"

"I liked the way you looked."

There was no mystery in her, she was as lacking in intrigue as a child. Anthony felt himself relaxing, the wind stroking his limbs, and the cries of the dark-skinned children, flashing in and out of the water like seals, rang pleasantly in his ears. He put out his hand and laid it carelessly on Diana's arm. The sun-warmed flesh made his fingers tingle slightly. He moved them up and down in an absent caressing way. "Where are you going, Diana? Who are you?"

She told him about herself, the uncomplicated story of a girl from an English country home, on a holiday trip halfway round the world. "We had some cousins in New Zealand, so I stayed with them for three months," she told him. "When I get home I'll have to get a job. Do you know anyone in England, Anthony?"

"Not yet. I've got several letters of introduction."

"Would you—come and stay with us? Oh, only if you're at a loose end, of course. We live in Dorset. The house is quite big, rather tumbledown. I've got a brother I think you'd like. And there's usually a horse to ride——" Her voice was soft and hurried, her face flushed with the sun or shyness, he didn't know which.

He was aware of his carefully maintained aloofness being invaded and was conscious of sudden resentment. But the warmth of the sun, the distant cries of the children, the splashing of the brilliant waves, made resentment too strenuous an emotion. He was filled with a drowsy peace. "That's very kind of you," he said. "I'd like to come."

It was Diana who jumped up later and said, "Come, we must hurry if we're to get back to Flora's Shop before the ship sails. I'd hate to miss it now. Actually——"

"Actually what?"

"There's something there I badly want." She picked up her beach bag and towel. "Hurry and dress. I'll meet you in five minutes."

It was already growing cooler. The fierceness of the day's heat had gone out of the burnt hills. As they came into the town and drove over the pontoon-bridge the tall narrow Dutch houses, cinnamon and peach-colored across the water, were scalloped against the sky. The big ships lay waiting for the bridge to swing aside, leaving them free to slide out of the harbor.

A sensation of panic filled Anthony. In less than an hour he, on board the larger waiting monster, would be leaving this place forever. And he hadn't yet seen Flora. In his haste he seized Diana's hand and pulled her through the crowded streets and alleyways. Skinny cats were still prowling. The paint flaked off the pink, yellow, and blue houses. Nobody swept the rubbish from the footpaths and dusty gardens. The sleepy dark Venezuelian sailors sat in their boats in the market place. Two black girls, pert, small-waisted, rolled their eyes expressively at Anthony.

Flora's Shop, at last reached, was a haven of luxury, of quiet, of civilization. But the door was still inexorably shut.

"She must be away," said Diana disappointedly. "Or perhaps ill."

Neither of those explanations pleased Anthony. He was so certain that Flora, elegant and remote, sat within, waiting for a voice or the touch of a hand to bring her suddenly to glowing life.

Was she really a mirage? Was the whole shop, with its alien air of culture, a mirage in the small, teeming, tropical town? Was it better, perhaps, for this overpowering dream of his to remain unrealized, one of the perfect unattainable things?

He became aware of Diana tugging at his hand. "Anthony, we'll have to go. Oh, I'm so disappointed."

"What was it you wanted in this shop?" Anthony asked, suddenly curious.

Diana pressed her small nose against the glass of the shop window.

"It was that mirror," she said, pointing to the gilt-framed mirror with its intricate frame of intertwining flowers and scrolls. "When I saw it this morning I had the silliest idea——" The faint color crept enchantingly into her cheeks again.

"What was the idea?"

"Oh, just that a mirror like that could only show a beautiful face. And that if I looked at myself in it I would really be as I wanted to be, lovely and delicate, like a face in an old painting."

As she stood there Anthony could actually see her face in the mirror, rosy with embarrassment, deliciously alive, perfectly framed with the rich golden curlicues. Why, he thought bewilderedly, not Flora but Diana is the lovely spirit in this shop. I caught a glimpse of her this morning in the mirror, but that was just a flash. Now she's here, dimpling and rosy and alive—*alive!*

Mixed with his sudden extraordinary happiness was the peace he had felt while lying in the sun on the beach. It enabled him to say gently, "Why do you want to be different, Diana?"

"Oh, because I'm quite ordinary."

She was young and vulnerable and unmysterious again, her friendly white cat look returned.

"If I said you were not ordinary—not to me, anyway—if I said I *liked* you being ordinary——" He was too eager, his words becoming confused.

But to Diana their confusion apparently made perfect sense, for her cheeks began to dimple, her eyes grew radiant. "Oh, Anthony, really? You don't hanker after a girl in a mirror? You like—*me?*"

He nodded.

She breathed deeply. "Oh, Anthony!" And then, "Heavens, it's so late—we must fly! It will never do to miss the ship."

"No, it will never do," Anthony cried, as urgent as she, as if it were life itself he might have been missing.


The sharp voice from upstairs could no longer be ignored. "Mina!"

"Yes, ma'am. I'se just opening the door."

A dusky finger pulled the bolt and the fading sunlight and a gust of warm wind came into the dark interior of the shop.

"I thought I heard people talking about the old gilt mirror. Were they customers?"

"Just passers-by, ma'am."

"Well, I'm coming down, anyway." There was the tap-tap of a stick and shuffling footsteps on the wooden stairs. Presently a thin, very old woman came slowly into view. Her back was bent, her hands knotted with arthritis. Her long, sunken-cheeked face was ruined with age, but it must always have been too large-featured for beauty. Now she looked querulous and suspicious. She made her slow way to the window and took out the mirror. Holding it in her knobby twisted hands she looked into the glass. An expression of distaste came over her face.

She sighed, then looked up suspiciously. "Mina! What are you standing there grinning for?"

The black woman's dark eyes moved guiltily away. But they retained their impression of the young rosy face in the mirror, the face that fitted so perfectly within the frame of the twining blossom—the face of youth.

She answered slowly in her rich, mirthful voice, "Dat ain't you in dat mirror, Miss Flora. Dat ain't you any more."

# Happy Ever After

While the house was full of workmen, Aunt Kitty stayed in her room, her eyrie as Anna called it, to escape the noise. In spite of rheumatism and eighty-eight years on her high-held white head, she insisted on keeping the room which had always been hers, even though it was up three flights of stairs.

Of course it would be difficult the day they had to carry her down, she said, but undertakers were paid to cope with that sort of thing. Anyway, she would no doubt die going about her usual affairs of the day, in the kitchen or the garden or the conservatory where the orange trees had died, but where there was still a healthy grapevine and a great variety of pot plants. Then all they would need to do would be to carry her into the library and prepare her there to meet her Maker.

Aunt Kitty talked a great deal about death, as of a friend who had neglected lately to call. Since taking Patrick, brave bonny Patrick, and later her sisters Dolly and Pauline, he seemed to have forgotten the McDermott family. And now he had better go on forgetting them until after Anna's ball. She was determined to see that.

So Valerie was left to cope with the workmen and all the preparations a fashionable coming-out ball involved.

Anna had been horrified when the idea had been broached to her. "Mother, you can't mean it! Not a coming-out ball for me; not for a working girl!"

"It's Aunt Kitty's idea," Valerie said apologetically. "It seems the McDermott girls have always come out. I'd have known more about this if your father had lived. But he didn't, and I think Aunt Kitty's remembering, too, that I missed my coming-out. The war was on then, and I got married and actually that was far more exciting than coming out."

"I can imagine," Anna said soberly, as if she, too, could remember those extraordinary years, which of course she couldn't. The war was over when she was born. And Patrick dead.

But her words reminded Valerie vividly of those long ago nights when the bombs were falling, and Patrick was with his squadron, and she alone was responsible for the three spinster aunts at Windrise. During the raids they had sat, Aunt Dolly, Aunt Kitty, Aunt Pauline and herself, in the kitchen, together with Hazel the cat, and a small suitcase which belonged, mysteriously, to Hazel.

They had sat there more for warmth than for safety,

the three aunts in their distinctly original night attire, very uptight, very unafraid, except that occasionally Aunt Dolly, the youngest, shivered violently, and immediately apologized.

They had been perfectly sweet to her, the newcomer, their nephew Patrick's so young bride. They had seemed to be looking after her instead of the way it was, she, a healthy competent young woman ready to organize three elderly women if the need arose. Fortunately the need didn't arise.

It was Patrick, not the women, who died, coming down in a blaze of glory and terror somewhere over Berlin only a month before the war ended. She never did discover what was in Hazel's suitcase which had not had to be put into use.

But Anna was protesting about the ball, saying how could they afford it, and anyway such junketings were obsolete. "I don't think you can disappoint Aunt Kitty," Valerie said. "She's eighty-eight, and that was her world. Balls, garden parties, picnics, Windrise. You know that Windrise will be sold when she dies. It will be the last junketing the old house will see. I think you've got to be graceful about it."

"These aren't graceful days," Anna protested. "Honestly, Mother, what will everyone say at the office? The others all live in bed-sitters and Earls Court and so on, and here's me having a grand ball."

She was so pretty, Patrick's daughter. She had his blue eyes and ebony lashes and an apple blossom skin of which even Aunt Kitty approved. But not his gay, ebullient nature. She was cool, quiet, immensely self-contained. She wouldn't hurt anybody in the world, but neither would she consent to a foolishness.

"You'd better go to Windrise and have it out with Aunt Kitty," Valerie said. "And then let me have a list of the people you want invited."

"You're assuming already that Aunt Kitty will win."

"Won't she?"

"It's time she stopped getting her own way. She must have bossed those poor sisters of hers disgracefully. No wonder they died off. If she wants to spend all that money on me I'd rather have a car."

"Tell her," Valerie suggested. "But in the meantime think of lists. And, darling, plenty of men. I won't be one of those hostesses who has to bribe young men to come."

"Nor me," Anna said feelingly. "And I like them in singles, not dozens."

"Oh, darling—is there one? Really?"

"*Mother!*" Anna exclaimed. "Honestly! Parents! Ancient aunts! All right, I'll go and see Aunt Kitty and talk her out of this folly." She didn't succeed, though. She came back, partly subdued, partly excited, and handed Valerie a list of names. "He's the most important," she said, pointing to the first one.

"Tim Brady," Valerie read. "Sounds Irish."

"Mother, do you honestly not remember?" Anna looked as Patrick had used to when he was feeling guilty about something. She met her mother's gaze with a brash bright stare.

"Should I?" Valerie said. "Tim? Tim Brady?"

"He was only the best man at your wedding!"

Her wedding . . . She was only nineteen and Patrick had twenty-four hours leave before joining his squadron.

It had been raining when they came out of church after the ceremony and Patrick had bought her a great armful of lilac from an old man with a barrow. The remembered fragrance of rain-washed lilac haunted her still. They had spent their brief ecstatic honeymoon near the airfield, in a country mansion that had been converted into a hotel. The bedroom had been immense, with an enormous four-poster bed, and she could still remember the pink hangings and soft rose-patterned carpet.

She was much older and had lived through many air raids with the three darling aunts, and was seven months pregnant with Anna, before Patrick was shot down over Berlin.

Try as she would she couldn't remember Tim Brady. Someone very tall standing beside Patrick. Dark hair, she thought. The uniform of a Fying Officer. She wasn't sure. She had had eyes for no one but Patrick. But she *must* remember for by one of those extraordinary coincidences one encountered in life, it seemed that Anna knew him all too well.

There was nothing wrong with that, of course. Except that he must be quite twenty years older than Anna.

Valerie knew that young girls often fell in love with men much older than themselves. She didn't have any strong feelings about that except that she had never imagined it happening to her own daughter. She was surprised at her violent reaction. "Anna, you can't be serious!"

"Serious, Mother?"

"About this Tim Brady. Why, he was your *father's* friend."

"That doesn't make him a leper," said Anna with her

infuriating calm. "Actually, he's very respectable. He's in the Foreign Office. Bowler hat and all that. He looks terribly sweet and distinguished. He got to be a Wing Commander, you know."

"But isn't he married?"

"No. All men aren't, you must know. And he's only thirty-nine."

"And you're eighteen."

"I'll age," said Anna. "If only I do it as nicely as you I won't worry. What are you going to wear to my ball, Mother?"

"So now it's your ball."

Anna sighed. "Aunt Kitty talked me into it, exactly as you knew she would. I suppose it might be quite fun. Mother, let me choose your dress."

"But I should be choosing yours."

"What a hope you've got! I'm going in something absolutely un-deb, or not at all. But I know you, you'll make me do with some horrid little discreet number to save money. If you must know, Aunt Kitty's given me a hundred pounds."

"*How* much?"

"It's to see that we—both of us—don't disgrace Windrise and family tradition and all that. So the responsibility's mine."

With the excitement of choosing dresses, and then the time spent at Windrise supervising alterations, not to mention arranging catering, flowers, music, invitations, Valerie had scarcely a moment, except those few frazzled ones before she fell asleep at night, to worry about Anna and her infatuation for a middle-aged man.

It was flattering that all the invitations were accepted,

and really rather moving the way the old house, with the freshening up the painters had given it, regained a semblance at least of its past graciousness. Since she had been widowed Valerie had gone back to her old job of being a florist so that now she was able, at a much reduced cost, to fill the hall and the ballroom with banks of flowers. All Aunt Kitty's clutter of old raincoats and boots and gardening equipment had been banished from sight, the floors polished, chandeliers taken down and washed to scintillating perfection, the splendid brocade curtains in the ballroom carefully cleaned and rehung so that the frayed and worn parts didn't show. The lawns were mowed, edges clipped, gravel paths raked. Old Mr. and Mrs. Murphy, who had taken care of Aunt Kitty and Windrise for years, were given positions of authority over the staff hired for the night. Mrs. Murphy had washed and starched to rigidity a cap and apron she hadn't bothered to wear for years, and Mr. Murphy forgot his lumbago and easily assumed the part of a dignified elderly butler.

This was the way Patrick had known Windrise. Valerie was too busy to have many moments of puzzlement that he didn't seem to be here, as she had expected he would be, with the past conjured up like this. Which was just as well, as she didn't want to be unhappy or too nostalgic at Anna's ball.

Aunt Kitty looked very splendid, as Valerie had known she would. Even leaning on her stick she looked very much the *grande dame* in her black velvet with the small ruffling of yellowed old lace, the rings (the ones she had left after selling the rest to pay for Dolly's and Pauline's funerals) glittering on her fragile fingers, a wisp of veil over her piled white hair, her fine eyes recapturing a youthful sparkle.

Beside her Anna, in spite of her radiant youth, looked almost austere. She had insisted on buying a white satin sheath which made her look pure and touchingly young. Valerie had demurred about it, thinking it too plain, too unadorned, but Anna had been so insistent that she hadn't dared demur about the dress Anna had chosen for her. Honey-gold chiffon.

It was a much more spectacular dress than Anna's. Valerie felt unhappy about it, and yet couldn't resist a thrill of pleasure when she put it on. It was a beautiful dress. She had never had anything so beautiful before. During the war there had been coupons and all those shortages, and since, with a not very profitable job and only Patrick's small amount of money left to her, she had concentrated on bringing Anna up to her best advantage. Besides, there had been no opportunities to wear such a dramatic dress.

One way and another, there had been just no time to meet Tim Brady. Once she had suggested that Anna might bring him to dinner one evening, but Anna had been offhand about that. "You'll meet him at the ball, Mother. Time enough." Was she a little embarrassed about him, after all? Did she want her mother to see him first in the heightened distinction of evening dress?

Well, that was the way he was to see her, too. First at her wedding, and then in this glorious golden chiffon. His future mother-in-law? It was really rather ludicrous.

The guests kept arriving, hordes of gay good-looking young people, a few friends of Valerie's and a handful of McDermott cousins, contemporaries of Aunt Kitty's, with elegant ravaged old faces and the fire still in their eyes.

Standing next to Aunt Kitty, Valerie shook countless hands, murmured greetings. She was aware of Anna nudging her. "Mother, it's Tim. *Tim!*"

She looked up, murmuring an apology. "So many people—I'm so glad to meet you," and was aware of the two grave eyes looking down at her. Serious contemplative dark eyes in a bony face of which even now she hadn't the faintest recollection. "You were Patrick's best man. Of course we've met before. Later we must talk."

"I'll look for you," he said.

She didn't see how Anna greeted him, for someone else was claiming her attention. Surely that gravity would lighten a little. Or did Anna, the daughter of laughing Patrick, like him that way?

It seemed she had scarcely entered the ballroom before he was at her side. "Dance? Or talk?"

Instinctively her eyes went over the couples on the dance floor, seeking for Anna. Hadn't she wanted to have her first dance with Tim? But Anna was dancing with a tow-headed young man Valerie hadn't remembered receiving really, she was getting worse and worse about faces, she must try to notice others besides those of the people she loved. "I'm sure I never looked as young as that," she said.

"Young? Oh, you're looking at Anna. She's lovely, isn't she? But you were just as young, you know."

"The day I married Patrick? Do you really remember? You make me ashamed to confess that I didn't even know who you were when Anna told me about you."

His serious eyes studied her. "Why should you? You were marrying Patrick."

"Yes. He had a way of claiming one's entire attention." She was realizing that after all these years she was at last able to talk about Patrick objectively. It was queerly comforting, as if she were being released from some spell, a wonderful spell but a little imprisoning and oppressive. Or was that feeling just the result of the music and the glass of champagne she had hurriedly swallowed after the ordeal of meeting so many guests, and the knowledge that she wore a beautiful dress and was in conversation with a good-looking man? Distinguished was the word Anna had used to describe him. He was Anna's. And perhaps more suitably so than she had imagined, for Anna had the same quality of seriousness. Only it was still a pity about the twenty years, never quite bridgeable, and Anna so radiantly young tonight.

Her thoughts were growing incoherent. She had, absurdly, to blink back tears. "Then shall we dance? I warn you I haven't for an awfully long time."

"Why not?" He meant his questions to be answered.

"I don't know. I just don't go out much. I work, and there's been Anna to bring up. Tonight is wild gaiety for me. It was Aunt Kitty's idea. I'm still not entirely sure whether she wanted to do it for Anna or to give herself the pleasure of reliving the past. She's such a darling. All Patrick's aunts were. You should have seen us during the air raids——"

It was easy to dance, after all. Or perhaps Tim Brady was rather good. "So I've been cherishing a myth about you," he said.

"What sort of myth?"

"Well, I thought there'd be all sorts of wonderful things for a girl like you, and here you've been spending your time looking after elderly women, and a child."

She laughed with amusement. "How funny! Did you think I'd be a gay widow?"

"Not at once. I realized Patrick wasn't easily forgettable. But after that—you're not exactly unnoticeable yourself."

Valerie laughed again. "If you're going to be gallant, so am I. I just can't think how I could have forgotten what you looked like. How have you filled in those twenty years yourself? You must have had to evade an awful lot of women."

"I was a man with an obsession."

"Yes? For your work?"

"Not exactly. That's a very lovely dress you're wearing."

"Anna chose it. She has wonderful taste for someone so young. She's really only young in appearance," she went on hastily. "In other ways she almost seemed to be born old. She's always found men of her own age much too young."

She felt her hasty attempt at approval and not hurting his feelings had been clumsy and inept, and was relieved to see him smiling. "I'd call them boys." He looked over his shoulder and added, "She seems to be making quite a good pretense of liking them."

Valerie caught a glimpse of Anna's face pressed gently against that of her partner, her eyes rapt, and was instantly deeply hurt for Tim's sake. "Oh, they do that, even with their bitterest enemy."

"Perhaps we should do the same."

For some unknown reason—it *must* be the champagne
—Valerie's heart gave a great leap. She drew back rather
sharply from the thin serious face momentarily so close
to hers. Then she was ashamed of her feeling of panic and
a moment later deeply relieved that the music was stopping. "It's too late. Anyway—I must be awfully old-
fashioned——" Would you dance like that with your
mother-in-law? she wanted to ask. Good heavens, was she
to be mother-in-law to this man who made her feel so
young, yes, really young. And attractive . . .

"Later," he said, and she reflected that that was a word
they were using a lot tonight.


Someone had put another glass of champagne in her
hand, and someone else, one of Anna's young men (or
boys, as Tim called them) was exclaiming in disbelief that
she could be Anna's mother. The band had started again,
and now Anna was dancing with Tim. But not cheek to
cheek. They were laughing and looked very happy and
animated. But not exactly intimate, Valerie thought. They
hadn't, or didn't show to the world, the intimacy of
lovers.

"It's a great success, isn't it?" Aunt Kitty was saying
in Valerie's ear.

"You mean—Anna and Tim?"

"No, no, no, the ball, child, the ball. It's like old times.
Windrise was built for this kind of thing. The Duke of
Wellington danced here, did you know? Just before he
left for the Peninsular War. And later Lord Castlereagh,
and once Disraeli, yes, would you believe it, the little
Dizzy with his black curls. And my two brothers before
they were killed at Mons. And Patrick . . . Well, when

I've gone you'll be finished with us, Valerie."

Valerie found herself unable to meet the old, too knowledgeable eyes. Just lately, yes, she could admit it tonight, she had wondered how marriage to Patrick would have worked out. She had the suspicion he might have grown too flamboyant for her, those constant high spirits and the necessity to live on excitement. How would they have settled into middle age?

"It's a lovely ball, Aunt Kitty," she said.

The old lady patted her hand. "I'm glad you've discovered you're not too aged and decrepit to dance. In another hour or two I'll cast away my stick and take a turn myself. The last of the mad McDermotts."

"No, Anna is the last," Valerie said.

"Anna is all yours, my dear. And bless her for it."

And that would be why Anna was attracted to a person like Tim Brady; because quiet sincerity appealed to her more than flamboyance. She realized that at the beginning of her life, whereas Valerie hadn't until—when? An hour ago? Twenty minutes ago, when Tim had held her in his arms to dance?

All at once the gaiety and happiness left her. Suddenly she was a little chilly, very sober, and afraid she was going to cry. There was a pain in her heart that she hadn't felt since the anguish of Patrick's many departures. She didn't even know why it was there. It was unreasonable, anti-social, gloomy, all the things she shouldn't be tonight.

"Mother!" Anna and Tim had danced close. "Tim says he can get seats for the new ballet. Isn't it wonderful?"

"I didn't know you cared so much for ballet," Valerie said automatically.

"No, but you do, Mother."

He doesn't need to please his mother-in-law, Valerie
wanted to say to Anna, but they had moved off, and she
found herself smiling at one of the unknown young men
who seemed to want to dance with her, really to want to.
Or else it was his exquisite manners, although she had
read that the young had no manners nowadays.

"Anna never told me she had such a beautiful mother,
Mrs. McDermott."

"Oh, tush. Thank you, though." She smiled, liking the
young honest face above her.

"I've been telling her she'd better look like you when
she gets older."

"Why, will it matter to you?"

"I hope so." His voice was puzzlingly fervent. He was
the boy Anna had been dancing cheek to cheek with,
Valerie realized. "I certainly hope so."

"One seems to spend an awful lot of time living on
hope," she said vaguely (and also trying not to hurt
people, she added to herself). "Isn't this a nice dance?
Anna's great-aunt arranged it. By the way, I must have
heard your name, but I'm awful both at names and faces."

"It's John Carruthers. And I hope you won't forget it,
Mrs. McDermott," he said earnestly.

"I'm sure I won't."

"Actually, I don't think you'll have the chance," said
the young man in his nice voice, but at that moment the
music changed and Valerie apologized, laughing, saying
this dance was something she hadn't yet had the opportunity to master. "But I'll probably manage before the
evening's over."

Tim Brady hadn't mastered it either. He asked permission to sit it out with Valerie while John Carruthers expertly took over Anna, and the two of them disappeared, laughing, among the noisy throng.

"It gives me a crick in my back," said Tim.

"Age," said Valerie, and realized that again she had said the wrong thing.

All the same Tim was looking at her with a twinkle. "I think I could manage to hobble in the garden. Could you?"

He was going to ask her if he could marry Anna—no, not ask her, tell her.

"I suppose I could. Oh, I didn't mean to seem ungracious, but the guests——"

"The guests are well launched. You can safely ignore them for the rest of the evening."

The electricians had hung extra lights along the terrace, but the lawns, the rose garden, the furbished-up border with the little sundial hung with ivy at the end, were in darkness. Tim, his arm tucked in hers, led her firmly away from the lights. "That's better," he said.

"It's rather dark. But peaceful. I must say that music sounds better from a distance."

"A very long distance."

"But Anna loves it." There she was saying the wrong thing again. "I suppose all young people do. I mean," she went on lamely, "it's a way of working off excess energy." And hurriedly, "Where did you and Anna first meet?"

"At a cocktail party given by my boss. She came with young John Carruthers."

"Oh, yes, the boy I was dancing with. And did you

recognize her at once? I mean, as mine and Patrick's daughter?"

"I saw the likeness to Patrick."

"She has his eyes. They're beautiful in a woman, aren't they?"

"Very. And would you mind, for just five minutes, stopping being Anna's mother?"

She hesitated. "But who am I? Patrick's wife?"

"Not Patrick's wife, either." There was a curious note, almost violent, in his voice. "Just a very beautiful woman, anonymous if you like, the way you were the first time I saw you. Patrick said to me, come and be my best man tomorrow, I'm getting married. So I went, and there you were, and you never once took your eyes off Patrick, and I never took mine off you—from that day to this."

"Tim!" Valerie gathered her senses. "But you never saw me again."

"In my mind I did. Always. I told you I was a man with an obsession."

"Tim!" she whispered it this time.

"I knew Patrick was dead, but I never found out what had happened to you. I knew I could if I tried." His hand was round hers. "Can I go on confessing?"

"Yes. No. Had you better?"

"I was afraid to set out to find out. I thought you'd have married again. I couldn't bear to know that. Or that you wouldn't see me, the way you didn't at your wedding. I suppose I took a long time to recover from the war. I had fairly bad back injuries, which explains why I can't do that devilish dance. Anyway, all those years went by, and then out of the blue I met Anna at a party."

Valerie carefully withdrew her hand. She did her utmost to make her voice gay, full of amusement at life's coincidences. "And you promptly fell in love with her in the same way! What a roundabout way to tell me, Tim dear. But I do understand."

She gave a gasp as she was spun round, his fingers biting into her shoulders. "You don't understand a thing. Valerie! Open those beautiful eyes of yours. Look at me! Read what's in my face, for heaven's sake!"

She couldn't speak for so long that she was afraid he would think her dumb. Or horrified. At last she whispered, "You idiot, it's too dark to see your face here. And if we go into the light you'll see that I'm—I'm c-crying."

She had forgotten, too, what it was like to be kissed in that way. Or she had never known, because Tim wasn't Patrick. His kiss was his kiss, not Patrick's. Afterwards, she was still crying. "Anna! Poor Anna!"

"Anna?" He sounded puzzled.

"You were top of the list. She said—she let me think she adored you."

"I hope she does. But she says she's going to marry John. Didn't you know?"

"John Carruthers! But she let me think—oh, be bothered to her! It's her father's guile. Tell me," she demanded, "how did she persuade you to come tonight?"

"By telling me her mother was still the most beautiful woman in the world."

"So she talked to Aunt Kitty—or Aunt Kitty talked to her——Now whose ball is this, anyway?"

"I think it's yours," Tim said. "I think the reason was that your Aunt Kitty had never got over you missing your coming-out because of the war."

"Now isn't that typical of the McDermotts!" Valerie cried. "Schemers! Wait till I have it out with Aunt Kitty!"

But when the ball was over, and everyone gone, Valerie asked Aunt Kitty something quite irrelevant. "I never did know what was in Hazel's suitcase. You remember, during the bombing."

"Oh, that was cat food. It was Dolly's idea. We knew how animals had had to suffer in the Irish famines. We didn't intend that to happen to Hazel. Funny——" The brilliant black eyes began to blur, "I remember those nights so well and yet I can't remember when Hazel died."

"Aunt Kitty—Tim Brady—he says he's in love with me."

The fine, sculptured old face still had its distant look. Aunt Kitty didn't seem to have heard what Valerie had said, for she was talking in a murmuring voice, as if to herself, "So many things to remember . . . One simply can't contain them all. It's better to forget a few. Even the ones one would imagine to be the most treasured . . ." Then Aunt Kitty, in her completely unpredictable way, snapped alive again. "So I hear Anna's to marry that Carruthers boy. Seems a gentleman."

"Does no one tell me anything?" Valerie cried. "Really, you and Anna! You've been conspiring. Who *was* this ball for tonight?"

"Tonight? This ball? The last at Windrise? Why, it was for the living, darling child."